Tribulation

Tribulation

Peter and Paul Lalonde

THOMAS NELSON PUBLISHERS®
Nashville

Published in Nashville, Tennessee, by Thomas Nelson, Inc.

Scripture references are from the following sources:

The KING JAMES VERSION of the Bible.

The REVISED STANDARD VERSION of the Bible. Copyright © 1946, 1952, 1971, 1973, by the Division of Christian Education of the National Council of the Churches of Christ in the U.S.A. Used by permission.

Library of Congress Cataloging-in-Publication Data

Lalonde, Peter.
    Tribulation / Peter and Paul Lalonde.
        p. cm.
    ISBN 0-7852-6729-8 (pbk.)
    1. Rapture (Christian eschatology)—Fiction. 2. End of the
world—Fiction. 3. Christian fiction. I. Title
    PS3562.A4147 T75 2001
    813'.54—dc21   00-46570
                                                           CIP

Printed in the United States of America

1 2 3 4 5 6 PHX 05 04 03 02 01 00

Preface

THE GREEN SPREADING BRANCHES of the majestic old oak cast cool shade on the gently rolling forest meadow. Birds sang happily from its height, and the sound of the wind in its leaves was like the pleasing murmur of children's voices.

In all its splendor and solitude the magnificent tree might have been the first thing to grow on God's green earth. Or it might have been the last—the lone survivor of a time after man had run his race. Ancient, eternal, the oak seemed to stand for everything that endured and abided. From generation to generation, epoch to epoch, it had stood a silent sentinel as kingdoms rose and fell around it, a solitary witness to the hopes and dreams, the fortunes and follies of mankind.

Yet, even now, on this glorious summer day with high white clouds making fanciful shapes in the pure blue sky, the tree served as welcome shelter for yet another generation—boys and girls who built birdhouses high in its canopy and swung like happy monkeys from its branches. Today, the mighty oak was a place of refuge and recreation, of peace and tranquillity. Today, three children—two kid brothers and their older sister—had come to this place to mark a moment of innocence and joy in their young lives. A moment to remember. A moment to cherish.

Tom and Calvin Canboro, their freckled faces brown from a day of play in the bright sunshine, watched with a mix of anticipation and wonder as their sister, Eileen, carefully carved an inscription into the gnarled bark of the tree with a pocketknife. Her face, framed in braided chestnut hair, was intent on her task, her tongue poking from one corner of her mouth, and she made sure each letter was perfectly spaced and cut deep enough into the living wood to last. Her eyes were dark and bright, her face splashed with the same sprinkling of freckles as her kid brothers, but unlike Tom and Calvin, ages eight and seven, respectively, Eileen at thirteen seemed much older and wiser than her years. It was as if she were aware of the precious quality of this fleeting moment; as if, deep in her spirit, she knew that this time would never come again and that their childhood was racing by like the clouds high above them.

Eileen Canboro had a special sensitivity, a way of seeing the world, that her rough-and-tumble brothers could only guess at. She knew, in the silent, unspoken places of her heart, that God had a plan for their lives—a plan that would test the bonds of family and the love they shared.

This time would not last forever, and neither would their innocence. It would be up to them, and to the Lord whom she had acknowledged at an early age, to keep faith with one another in the trials and tribulations to come.

That same faith was mirrored in the very words Eileen carved into the tough hide of the tree, a reflection of her belief that, whatever might come, they would always find a safe haven in the love and loyalty that forge a special link between brothers and sisters. Even as she worked, she cast a protective eye to Calvin and Tom, noting the way they looked up to her, simple trust in their clear blue eyes, the unquestioning expectation that their big sister would be there for them, no matter what. After all, that's what family was all about.

Still concentrating carefully on her work, she couldn't help smiling as she noticed her brothers squirming from the corner of her eye. For them, as for every child, patience was a virtue that must be learned, then nurtured. *Good things come to those who wait, and in God's time,* Eileen thought. Good things were coming. Of that, she was sure.

Tom finally gave voice to the brothers' restlessness. "Come on, Eileen," he cajoled. "What's taking so long?"

"Yeah, Eileen," Calvin echoed in precisely the same tone of voice. "What's taking so long?"

"Almost done," Eileen cheerfully replied. "You two will just have to hang on for a sec."

"That's what you said twenty minutes ago," Tom replied with a shake of his head.

"Yeah," repeated the copycat Calvin. "That's what you said twenty minutes ago."

Eileen continued carving, even as she answered her brothers with an indulgent smile. Everything, she knew, could be a lesson in life if you looked at it the right way.

Today, she hoped her brothers would learn that, from God's point of view, one minute could be a million years . . . and a million years, one minute.

"Hey," she said, gently scolding, "we want this to last, don't we? If it's going to be around awhile, we've got to take the time to make it right."

Tom looked skeptical. "I don't know about that," he said. "But I do know that if we don't hurry up and get home, Calvin's going to wet himself."

"Yeah," Calvin piped in. "If we don't hurry up—" It was only then that he realized what his brother had said and he narrowed his eyes, glaring at Tom in a mixture of confusion and exasperation.

Eileen stifled a laugh. Her brothers could be more entertaining than a circus act. But she knew better than to keep them waiting much longer. She wanted their full attention for what she was about to show them and tell them.

Folding her knife and slipping it into the pocket of her flowered print dress, Eileen stepped back. "Ta da!" she sang out in two musical notes, and her brothers crowded close to get a good look at her handiwork. The inscription was elegant but simple, carved with a sure hand and a steady eye:

Eileen, Calvin, and Tom Canboro
July 1961

"That's real pretty," said an admiring Tom.

"Yeah," added Calvin, "real pretty." This time, though the words were the same, the feeling was his own.

"It's more than just pretty," Eileen said, and her brothers could tell from the tone of her voice that she had something serious on her mind. "I put this here for a very special reason."

"What is it?" they asked at once, their eyes widening as if they were about to be let in on a deep secret.

"I want you both to listen very carefully," Eileen replied, taking a step toward them and putting a hand on each boy's shoulder. "I know how you both like to play around this old forest after school and on the weekends. And it's a wonderful place to play, that's for sure. But, you know, sometimes Mom gets afraid that you'll stray too far . . . you'll get lost and won't be able to find your way back."

"Nah," interjected Tom with all the confidence of an eight-year-old. "We know our way around."

"Yeah," Calvin parroted. "We know our way around."

"That's as may be," Eileen continued, again trying not to smile, "but you know Mom. She worries. So I told her I'd make sure we'd have a place where we could meet up in case anything ever happened and we got separated." She squeezed their shoulders. "You know, just in case."

She looked up at the green canopy of the oak, and the gaze of her brothers followed. "This is the place," she said solemnly. "This is the tallest tree hereabouts, and you can see it for miles around. This is where I want you boys to come, should you ever need to."

Tom and Calvin nodded, captured for a moment by the grown-up tone in their sister's voice. They might not have been exactly sure why she was telling them all this, but if it was important to her, well then, it was important to them also. It had to be. Eileen was their big sister. She'd always looked out for them. And she always would.

But, as always, their boyish attention spans were almost immediately drawn away from the earnest scene being played out in the shadows of the tree and onto the prospect of an afternoon of adventure.

"Can we go now?" asked Tom.

"Yeah," Calvin once more echoed, his words almost running into his brother's. "Can we go now?"

Eileen shook her head, and from the look in her eyes, both boys knew that she was still intent on the plan and purpose that had brought them here. "There's one more thing," she said and, reaching out, she took them both by the hand. "I think you know what it is. Let's close our eyes."

Tom cast a quick glance at Calvin and rolled his eyes. They certainly did know what was coming next. For the life of them, they couldn't understand why their sister, so sensible in every other respect, was always insisting on saying a prayer, talking to Someone they couldn't see, just as if He were actually there. It seemed a little strange and spooky to Tom and Calvin, the way Eileen had of speaking out to God and telling Him what she wanted. As far as the two boys were concerned, God might have made the whole world and everything in it, but if they couldn't see, feel, or hear Him, what good was He?

Though neither of them would dare to speak out his doubts, Tom managed to sneak a frustrated look to his brother, rolling his finger at his temple in the time-honored sign of crazy behavior. It was only when he caught sight of his sister's glare that he settled down, bowed his head, and closed his eyes.

Eileen cleared her throat, and when she spoke, her voice was clear and confident, rising up above the chirping of the birds and the rustle of leaves in the wind. Whether or not Tom and Calvin believed, there had never been a question in her young mind that every prayer she spoke was heard and answered.

"Dear God," she began, "please protect this tree. Let it stand tall and proud forever. Let it be a beacon for us if we ever lose our way. Let this be the place that we come to when we really need someplace safe." She paused, then squeezed her brothers' hands. "Well," she concluded, "I guess that's it. Thank You, God. Amen."

She opened her eyes and was greeted by a smug look from Tom. "I told you," he said triumphantly.

"What?" Eileen asked. "What did you tell me?"

"I told you it was taking too long."

Eileen followed Tom's gaze to the crotch of Calvin's shorts where a wet stain had begun to grow. He had a puddle at his feet and a sheepish look on his face.

Chapter 1

SUNSHINE POURED THROUGH THE WINDOWS, glancing off the bright white enamel of the appliances and bringing a bright and cheerful glow to the kitchen. With the coffeemaker merrily percolating and the delicious aroma of homemade bread wafting through the room, it was a welcoming place, a casual rendezvous for old friends and close relations.

On a shelf near the tiled counter where Tom Canboro leaned sipping his morning coffee, a row of family photographs was displayed—Fourth of July picnics and Christmas dinners; Hawaiian holidays and anniversary celebrations. Each photo encapsulated a memorable moment in a happy and fulfilled life.

Among the keepsakes was a framed magazine cover featuring two attractive women smiling into the camera beneath a headline that had read "We're #1" before someone had crossed out the first word and replaced it with "Weird." Below the portrait bold-faced text proclaimed, "Aliens, Demons & Psychics Mean Big Ratings!" The cover was obviously a proud souvenir of success for a media-savvy broadcast professional.

But the picture that had caught Tom's attention was an aging black-and-white one in a silver frame. In it, three children—two brothers and their older sister—posed in front of a stately oak where, just visible behind them, were names carved deep into its bark. As Tom picked up the relic from his childhood and looked closely at it, the memory of those days came flooding back, and he laughed, remembering again the simple joy of being young.

A big, strapping man in a tracksuit, with a ready smile and a head full of blond hair, Tom moved with easy assurance, content with himself and the trappings of the good life that surrounded him. His blue eyes flashed with the merriment of his memories, and the sound of his laughter was pleasant and infectious, a reflection of his generous, open, and engaging personality. Simply put, Tom Canboro was a man content with his lot in life, self-sufficient and fully confident of his own abilities to handle any situation, come what may.

Still laughing, he handed the picture over the counter to his wife, Suzie, busy slicing a fragrant loaf of bread, fresh from the oven. Like her husband of ten years, Suzie exuded the confident and competent air of a person who had accomplished a lot in her life and expected to accomplish a lot more. Her honey blonde hair was cut shoulder length, and even in the casual clothes she wore, a simple elegance about her made it easy to like this attractive and intelligent woman. Small wonder she was featured on the framed magazine cover among the other photos—Suzie Canboro was a natural for a high-profile job in television.

Taking the picture from Tom's hand, she joined in his laughter. "Now," she said, "are you sure about that?"

"Absolutely," replied Tom, looking at his wife with affection that seemed to grow with time. "I remember it like it was yesterday. We had been out at that tree for hours, and poor little Calvin just couldn't hold it anymore." He guffawed, adding, "It didn't take more than a minute for him to be standing in a puddle."

"Now wait a minute!" protested a voice from across the room. "That never happened. I never wet myself. That's just an old family legend!"

Sitting at the kitchen table, Calvin joined in the fun at his expense. What he lacked in the personality and powerful assurance of his brother, Calvin made up for with a good-natured smile and a comfortable informality that reflected his easygoing nature. Even in the face of his brother's ribbing, Calvin's exasperation was only an act. Like the others gathered in Tom and Suzie's kitchen that morning, he knew teasing was one way friends and family expressed their love for one another. Right now, he might have been the target for their jokes, but the tables could turn in a minute, especially when they knew one another, their strengths and weaknesses, hopes and dreams, foibles and follies, so well.

He turned to another familiar face, seated across from him at the table. "Tell them, Eileen," he pleaded. "That never happened, did it? Tom's just making it up."

Eileen took a sip of her coffee and smiled. Although the oldest of the siblings, she still retained the gleam in her eye that had marked her from childhood. Eileen had grown gracefully into middle age, taking with her the gentle but firm authority that had made her a big sister to be respected. It was clear for those with eyes to see that, from the strength of character shining through in her face, the abiding faith Eileen had never been without had grown and matured as she reached adulthood, becoming the steady and unshakable foundation of her life. But it was equally clear that this faith had been, more than once, a point of contention with those to whom she was the closest. For Eileen, believing had come at a cost, a cost she counted every time she confronted the self-assurance and pride of her younger brothers.

"To tell you the truth, Calvin," she said. "I've heard Tom's version so many times now that it's hard to remember what actually did happen that day."

Calvin's insistent cries and Tom's renewed laughter filled the sunlit kitchen. There, on that pristine morning, on a suburban street that could have been in any of a hundred comfortable and well-tended American neighborhoods, life went on in the same timeless rhythms it had sustained since creation was breathed into being. And anyone who might have happened onto the happy scene might well have thought that the world would continue to turn as it always had. Day would turn into night and back again to morning, waking people just like this, who would begin their days safe and secure in the knowledge that nothing could ever disturb their routines that carried them across the span of their lives.

But in another part of the Canboro household such assurances were harder to come by. Even as the shouts and laughter from the kitchen echoed through the spacious and comfortable home, reaching down into a converted basement bedroom, other certainties were beginning to make themselves felt. Those certainties insisted that, however long this present world had gone on from day to day and year to year, the time was coming when everything, in the twinkling of an eye, would be thrown over and changed forever. That time was fast approaching, the whispered voices from the basement seemed to be saying. The day of reckoning was closer than anyone might have imagined.

Hunched over a card table, a trembling figure could almost hear those whispers above the hum of the air conditioner and the faint voices from above. Dark-haired and dark-eyed, with an earring piercing one lobe and a goatee gathered at his chin, Jason Quincy stared at the board in front of him decorated with strange symbols and an alphabet written out in Gothic script. His fingers resting lightly on a small planchette, he watched it move as if powered by some invisible hand, around the board, moving closer, ever closer to the number 6.

When the Ouija board pointer finally reached its destination, hovering over the numeral, Jason pulled back his fingers as if he had brought them too close to a flame. Grabbing a pen from the piles of paper and open books spilling out onto the floor around him, he scribbled down the last notation of the message he had received, nodding to himself, his eyes wide with a mixture of fear and wonder as he read the notation "Genesis 11:6."

Quickly he turned pages in the books, looking for something—a clue, a confirmation—to what he was being told. He scanned volumes of UFO lore, accounts of alien abduction, and historical studies of witchcraft, magic, and sorcery with avid attention. But a single well-worn book held Jason's eyes the longest as he traced the lines of type with a trembling finger. *Babel Becomes One* was its haunting title, but even those words could not do justice to the mesmerizing stare of its author on the back cover. *Franco Macalousso* was the author's byline, and the look with which he fixed his worldwide readership was both strange and compelling. There was an undoubted charisma to the man's chiseled features, and his smile seemed to promise friendship and understanding in boundless measure.

Yet even as Jason stared at the photo for the ten-thousandth time since one of Macalousso's disciples had handed it to him on the street, he could hear, if only faintly, some still, small voice in the back of his mind crying out a warning. The doubt and uncertainty between that welcoming smile and the distant voice from deep inside sometimes made Jason wonder whether he was actually going crazy.

Suddenly, as if waking from a trance, Jason became aware of the people upstairs, just over his head. *Perhaps,* he thought, his mind turning in tighter and tighter circles, *perhaps they can help me make sense of it all. That is, if it's not already too late.* Those words themselves seemed to come from outside his fevered brain, and frightened by the sensation that he was not alone, Jason rose and hurried up the flight of creaking wooden stairs.

The dark dreariness of the basement seemed a world away from the sun-dappled expanse of the kitchen where the easy banter of the morning continued. Tom was finishing his coffee while Suzie took a bite of her delicious bread, sharing the bounty with her brother- and sister-in-law.

"So tell me," Eileen was saying to Suzie as she helped herself to a warm slice, "has Tom ever taken you out to that old tree of ours?"

Suzie nodded and smiled. "Occasionally," she replied. "It's his favorite spot for . . ."—she paused, making sure her husband was paying attention to her next words—"anniversary picnics."

Tom looked back at her blankly. Suzie was still trying to decide whether he had forgotten their special day or was just bluffing as he sometimes did to keep her guessing when Jason burst into the kitchen. All conversation stopped, and Suzie watched her brother make his way to a window looking out on the street and peek through the curtains as if expecting unwelcome company at any moment. Eileen, Calvin, and Tom stared at his bizarre behavior, but the disturbed Jason hardly seemed to notice as he peered up into the cloudless blue sky. The look in his bulging eyes seemed to suggest that at any moment alien spacecraft would descend onto the front lawn.

"Um," Suzie ventured tentatively, "is . . . everything all right, Jason?"

The nervous tension that seemed to emanate from Jason like heat from a furnace was cranked up several notches by his sister's question. Turning from the window, he fixed her with a frightened gaze. "All right?" he repeated, his voice cracking. "Of course everything is all right. Why shouldn't it be? Is there something you're not telling me?"

"No," Suzie replied soothingly, "of course not." She threw a concerned look in her husband's direction. "It's just that . . . well, we haven't seen you for a few hours, that's all."

Jason's eyes darted around the room, taking in the others' faces for the first time. One by one they smiled back at him, doing their best to appear as friendly and reassuring as possible. Slowly Jason began to relax, his hunched shoulders dropping and his eyes returning to their sockets.

"I'm fine, Sis," he said. "Just fine. I was . . . thirsty. That's all." Crossing to the refrigerator, he pulled out a bottle of water and, unscrewing the cap with a violent twist, gulped down the cold liquid. Careful to appear nonchalant, Jason had begun to move toward the dining room door when he stopped dead in his tracks, transfixed by the sight of something on the chair near Eileen.

"What's that?" he asked, pointing with a trembling finger.

"It's my purse," replied a mystified Eileen.

"No!" Jason was almost shouting now. "Inside it! What's that inside it?"

Eileen reached over and pulled out the pocket-size Bible that had been sticking out the top of her handbag. "It's a Bible," she said, holding it out and flipping through the pages. "See, Jason? The Bible?"

In the next moment Jason's fear turned to fascination as he took a step toward Eileen and asked in a hoarse whisper, "Can I ask you something?"

"Of course, Jason," Eileen replied. "Anything."

"What . . . ," Jason said, his voice catching on the words, "what does it say in Genesis 11:6?"

Eileen thought for a moment. "If I'm not mistaken, that's a passage about the Tower of Babel." She thumbed through the well-worn index tabs. "Why do you ask?"

"No reason," Jason answered, his paranoia returning. "I just thought it might . . . be important."

"Everything in this book is important," Eileen said with utter certainty, even as from the seat next to her, Calvin rolled his eyes in Tom's direction. Although Eileen saw the silent exchange between her brothers, she let it pass. *Never mind,* she told herself. *Everything happens in God's good time.* She continued turning through the scripture, finding the passage early in the book and reading it aloud.

"Okay," she said. "Chapter eleven, verse six. 'And the LORD said, "Behold, they are one people, and they have all one language; and this is only the beginning of what they will do; and nothing that they propose to do will now be impossible for them."'" She looked back to Jason. "Is that what you were interested in?"

Jason seemed to hardly hear her, his eyes fixed instead on a point faraway from the homey kitchen, far beyond the reach of family and friends. "Macalousso," he breathed. "Franco Macalousso was right." The tremor in his voice seemed to express a strange combination of fear and certainty as if he had heard words that confirmed some terrible event yet to happen.

There was silence in the kitchen for a long moment before a puzzled Calvin spoke up. "Franco Maca-who?" he asked.

"Franco Macalousso," Jason repeated as if uttering a forbidden name.

Suzie nodded. "You know, Calvin," she said. "He's the head of the European Unity Project."

Eileen gave a snort of derision. "Oh, please," she said with disgust. "Franco Macalousso wouldn't know a Bible if he got hit in the head with one."

Jason leaned across the table, his face very close to hers. "You don't understand," he hissed. "Franco Macalousso doesn't *need* the Bible. He's got something better . . . far better. He's got the truth. Don't you see?" he continued, staring deep into Eileen's eyes with frightening intensity. "We're all capable of doing the exact same miracles that God, that Jesus, did. And more." He pulled back, holding his finger high in the air as though proclaiming from a podium. "But first we've got to come together."

Eileen shook her head sadly. "That's what they thought when they built the Tower of Babel, Jason," she said, holding the open Bible up to him. "But they were wrong. Unity isn't the answer. It's not even—"

"And you wonder why the world is full of hate and war," Tom interrupted, cutting off his sister with a cold and suddenly hostile tone of voice.

"Yeah," Calvin piped in as if they were once again little

boys. "How can anyone be opposed to unity? I mean, without unity, what chance is there of ever having world peace?"

"Let me guess," Tom interjected, with no attempt to hide his scorn. "This Macalousso guy is really a Communist. Right, Sis?"

Eileen just shook her head. Sometimes patience was the greatest virtue of them all. "Not exactly," she said, taking a deep breath and mentally counting to ten. "Go ahead," she continued, turning to Jason. "Why don't you tell them exactly how Macalousso is going to go about achieving world unity."

From across the room Suzie was gesturing silently to Eileen with a simple, urgent message: don't go there. But it was too late.

More than ready to explain his fascination with the charismatic world figure, Jason spoke rapidly, his voice at a high pitch. The gathering in the kitchen cast quick, concerned glances to one another. There was no stopping him, and there was nothing left to do but let him have the floor.

"It's not a theory," Jason insisted, gathering a head of steam. "Not even close. It's scientifically proven. Every last word of it."

"Well, come on, then," said Calvin, drawing dirty looks from the others. "Share it with the ignorant."

"I will," Jason proclaimed. "And I'll share it with the rest of you too."

The joke brought the momentary relief of laughter, but the tension in the room quickly returned as Jason continued his intense monologue.

"Let me ask you something, Calvin," he was saying. "Have you ever heard of Dr. Emil Fugomoto?"

"Can't say as I have," Calvin admitted.

"How about the Isle of Manchi?" Jason asked. The look in his eyes behind the thick lenses of his glasses only magnified his fervor.

"Look," said an exasperated Calvin. "What's all this got to do with Franco Macalousso and world peace?"

"I'm getting to that," insisted Jason. "See, there is a reason you haven't heard of these places and these people. It's because they just happen to be part of one of the most important discoveries in the history of the world. But"—and here he held up his fingers in imaginary quotation marks— "the 'powers that be' have been working overtime to keep it all quiet."

"Just what kind of discoveries are you talking about, Jase?" asked Tom, intrigued in spite of himself.

"Yeah," echoed Calvin out of a habit born in childhood. "What kind of discoveries?"

If it was possible, Jason's excitement level seemed to rise even higher at the prospect of having people actually listening to him. "Big ones," he said in a hoarse whisper. "Very big ones. Just listen to this."

With a conspiratorial air, he sat down at the table, talking in a voice so low the others had to lean forward to hear him. As he did so, Tom caught the look of concern on his wife's face and smiled reassuringly. He's harmless enough, her husband's expression seemed to say.

"As part of his research," Jason continued, acting for all

the world like a spy in a James Bond movie, "Dr. Fugomoto traveled to an island to study the behavior of monkeys. But, you see, this wasn't just any ordinary island. No. The Isle of Manchi was divided almost exactly in half by a huge volcanic mountain."

With a violent gesture, shocking in its disregard for the peaceful morning setting of the kitchen, Jason thrust out his arm and with a clean sweep cleared the table of food, dishes, and utensils. He sent everything clattering to the floor where spilled milk and coffee mixed to form a large light brown puddle floating with cereal flakes and pieces of fruit. Only by a quick reflex action was Calvin able to rescue his mug. For a long moment nobody moved as all of them realized the potential for random violence behind Jason's heightened emotional state.

Almost before anyone had a chance to recover, Jason grabbed a sweater draped over the back of a chair and, twirling it into a loose length, laid it across the table. "See," he said triumphantly. "It was just like this. Cut right straight down the middle. There was no way to get from one side to the other. Not without sailing around the island or flying over it in a helicopter. And," he added with a knowing look, "monkeys don't sail and they don't fly choppers."

"So what was the experiment all about?" asked Eileen cautiously.

"I'm getting to that," replied Jason with a rapid stutter. Grabbing a banana off the floor, he set it down on one segment of his imaginary island, then stood back to admire his handiwork. "Now, on this side of the island, Dr. Fugomoto and his team laid out pieces of fruit to coax the monkeys from the forest so that they could study them. But what do you think their first problem was?"

He looked around the room where one by one, he was met with shrugs and shaking heads.

"They had to peel the fruit, of course," he continued a bit impatiently, "so that the monkeys could smell it and be tempted to come out of hiding."

His next act was almost as strange as his table-clearing demonstration. Looking quickly around the room, he caught sight of a Rice Krispies square lying where he had knocked it to the floor. Crushing the bar in his trembling hands, he spread out the crumbs across the table and, within moments, had peeled the banana and rolled it in the rice particles until it was well coated. He held it up for the others to see.

"The problem for Dr. Fugomoto, not to mention the monkeys," he explained, "was that they ended up eating more sand than fruit. That is until, one day, one smart monkey—one very smart monkey—figured out a way to clean his food before he ate it." Demonstrating, Jason dipped the crumb-covered banana in Calvin's cup of coffee, causing a cry of protest that he completely ignored.

"Smart monkey," he repeated, holding up the peeled banana, free from rice particles but now dripping with coffee. Jason looked smug and self-satisfied with his presentation. He was definitely on a roll. "Well, it didn't take long for his fellow monkeys to catch on, and before you knew it, half of the island had monkeys dipping their lunch in the sea."

Calvin, about to take a sip of the coffee, suddenly

remembered what it had been used for and pushed it away with a distasteful look. "Okay," he said. "So what does that prove? Monkey see, monkey do?"

Jason looked around the room as if aware that others might be listening through the walls. "Oh, there's a lot more to it than that," he said, his voice even lower now. "A whole lot more. See, there came a point in the experiment, after lots and lots of monkeys were cleaning off their food the way they'd seen it happen the first time, that another monkey arrived on the beach from out of the jungle." With two fingers, he walked the imaginary simian across the tabletop. He continued, "Naturally, he saw what the others were doing and decided to give it a try. Only this time"—he looked around the room as if anticipating the amazement they would experience after his earth-shaking revelation— "something incredible happened. At the very instant that this new monkey tried out the food-cleaning technique, the monkeys on the other side of the island"—and he slammed his hand down loudly on the far side of the table, causing the puzzled gathering to jump—"those monkeys started doing exactly the same thing."

"Really?" asked Tom with genuine fascination.

"Oh, yes," Jason reassured him. "It's all been documented. But that's not all."

"There's more?" said Suzie warily.

"There certainly is," responded her brother. "Because, you see, as soon as that one monkey cleaned off his food, that special ability was passed on not just to the other side of the island, but to monkeys all around the world."

"Now that's cool," said an impressed Tom.

"Oh, it's way more than cool," replied Jason. "It's absolutely incredible." He turned to look at the others, fixing them with his magnified stare, one after the other. "Think of the possibilities," he told them. "Just imagine if we could get enough people to think about a world at peace, a world without war, all at the same time." His eyes continued to search their faces as if inviting them, in that very moment, to join with millions of others in hearing the same wonderful dream. "Think about it," he repeated as he tapped his forehead and stood up to leave.

The others watched him silently as he crossed the room, turning in the doorway and nodding his head as if his certainty had suddenly grown into a passionate conviction.

"Franco Macalousso has it right," he announced. "If we can all just find a way to come together as one . . . then, whatever we believe, we can achieve."

With those words he disappeared down the hall, leaving a sense of foreboding behind him in the bright white reaches of the sunny kitchen.

Chapter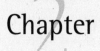

T OM BROKE THE LONG SILENCE that followed after
Jason left the room. Even as Suzie wet a sponge and
crossed to the mess her brother had made to clean it up, the
solemn look on her husband's face stopped her.

"I'm telling you, Honey," Tom said, his voice conveying
all the gravity he felt, "I love your brother. You know that. But
Jason is a guy who needs some serious professional help."

"No way," Suzie replied, shaking her head adamantly.
"I refuse to let those idiots at the psych ward near him
again. He was doing just fine until they started pumping
him full of drugs."

"Fine?" Tom said, trying hard to keep his incredulity
under control. "Fine? Get real, Honey. Don't you remember last Christmas?" He turned to the others to explain. "He
spent an entire week trying to convince us that the UN had
been taken over by alien invaders."

"He's much better now," Suzie insisted. "You know he
is."

Tom recoiled as if he couldn't believe his ears. Yet, even as he argued with his wife, he knew her love for her brother was as stubborn and unshakable as his own for Calvin and Eileen. He was only trying to do what was right for them and for Jason.

"Maybe you didn't just hear the same thing I did," he said to her. "He's actually convinced that if he can get enough people to agree with his crazy ideas, then one day we'll all wake up believing"—he swallowed hard with frustration—"whatever it is he believes."

"Okay," responded an equally frustrated Suzie. "So he has a rich imagination. What's wrong with creating a world that he can enjoy . . . a world that he can believe in?"

It was a standoff, watched by an increasingly uncomfortable and embarrassed Calvin and Eileen. It was the sort of private family situation that should be worked out behind closed doors between a husband and a wife. The thick tension was broken by the jingling of the telephone down the hall in the living room.

"I'll get it," said Suzie, thankful to find a way out of bickering with her husband.

After she left, Calvin turned to his brother and sister, making a sign that instantly summed up his feelings about the situation: a finger twirled above his head like a halo. "Sometimes Jason sounds like some of your born-again buddies, Eileen."

"Well, Calvin," his sister shot back, "you haven't got a thing to worry about then. Because if ignorance is bliss, you're already on the other side of the Pearly Gates."

Tom laughed out loud at the comeback, relieved that the problem of his brother-in-law had been put aside for the moment. He was quickly joined by his siblings. *It feels like old times*, he reflected, the three of them laughing together.

Moving to a comfortable armchair by the television, Suzie picked up the phone even as she heard the sound of the Canboro brood down the hall. *They're just like a bunch of grown-up kids*, she thought with an affectionate shake of her head as she clicked on the phone.

From the background noise over the receiver, she knew immediately the caller's identity and where she was calling from. The sound of techs and stagehands hustling and bustling in the high-ceilinged expanse of the WNN television studios was the only clue she needed. It had to be Helen Hannah, her partner for the award-winning investigative program that was celebrated in the framed picture in the kitchen.

"Hello, Helen," she said. "What's up?"

The pleasant, clear, and authoritative voice at the other end of the line laughed. "What are you," asked Helen Hannah, "one of those psychics we're always interviewing? Maybe we should do a show on you."

It was Suzie's turn to chuckle. "Actually," she said, "I've been expecting your call. Did you get my message?"

"The one about the Bible prophecy guy?" asked the voice from the studio. "I sure did. So, what's his story anyway? Is he predicting some fire from heaven that's going to destroy all mankind? That would sure be a scoop."

"Better than that," replied Suzie. "It seems this guy is claiming that millions of people are going to suddenly vanish off the face of the earth. And he says the Bible backs him up . . . all the way."

There was a pause as Helen tried to absorb this startling piece of information. "Let me get this straight," she said. "Millions of people are just to disappear in a puff of smoke?"

"That's the story."

The silence on Helen's end of the line conveyed her skepticism better than any words. "He must be talking about their souls or something, right?" she said at last.

"That's what I thought," Suzie admitted. "But that's not it at all. Apparently the whole person is gone . . . body and all." She leaned into the phone, her newshound instincts sharply attuned. "But that's not the best part," she continued in a confidential tone. "It seems that every Christian actually believes this. Every real Christian, that is."

"Really?" Now Helen was beginning to sniff a headline-grabbing story.

"Really," replied Suzie. "They've even got a name for it. It's called—" She stopped, trying to remember, then cupped her hand over the receiver and shouted back toward the kitchen.

"Hey, Eileen," she cried, "what's that book of Revelations thing you're always talking about where everyone's going to disappear?"

"It's called the Rapture" came the answer from across the house. Suzie started to relay the information to her partner but was interrupted by Eileen, still calling out from the kitchen. "And it's not all the people," she was saying. "It's just the real Christians. And it's not the book of Revelations. It's the book of Revelation."

"Thanks," said Susie, rolling her eyes. "Did you get all that?" she asked.

Back in the kitchen, Calvin was continuing to have fun at Eileen's expense. "Wow!" he was saying after Eileen had answered Suzie's shouted question. "Some of the stuff you guys believe really freaks me out. I mean, you're getting to sound more and more like Jason every day."

Tom, who had been only too willing to join in with Calvin to tease Eileen, frowned at the mention of his brother-in-law's name. "Poor Jason," he said with genuine feeling. "I love the guy with all my heart, you both know that, but I just can't help but think that he's going to be better off in a home or a hospital or something. Someplace where they can take care of him. I mean, a good imagination is one thing. But this guy is way beyond imagining. He actually believes the stuff he's talking about."

Eileen's smile mirrored all the comfort and understanding that a big sister naturally has for her younger siblings. "I think he just needs something to comfort him," she suggested. "Maybe if he knew God—"

"Wait just a minute there, Sis," interrupted Calvin, holding up his hand. "I think you're way off base with all that religious talk. Jason is one guy who has plenty of imaginary friends to play with. God would just be one more to freak him out."

Calvin turned to his brother. "Help me out here with something, would you, Tom? Why is it that people who claim to talk to little green men from Mars are considered insane and locked away, while people like our own dear sister here, who claim to talk to God, are somehow right as rain? Correct me if I've got this wrong, but I fail to see the difference. I really do."

"That's because you've never looked," responded Eileen with a clarity and power that stopped both brothers short. "Neither one of you has. And I just hope you get around to asking the right questions before it's too late."

"You mean before all you good Christians disappear," said Calvin, his voice dripping with sarcasm.

Tom shook his head ruefully. That was always the way between brothers and sisters—fussing and feuding and, underneath it all, a love that no words could express. He walked over to a small safe in a cabinet above the refrigerator, dialed the combination, and pulled out a badge, a police service revolver, and a regulation shoulder holster. He closed the safe door, leaving a second gun behind.

"Well," he said as he inspected his equipment, "I'd love to stay and continue this friendly family chat, but unfortunately a whole city full of people out there can't look to God or a clean banana or whatever when they're being hustled and harassed by every lowlife that crawls out from under a rock." He checked his revolver, spinning the chamber before slipping it into its holster. "Sometimes," he added, looking at them, "blind faith just isn't enough." He slipped the badge into the breast pocket of his T-shirt beneath his tracksuit, even as Eileen reached out and put her hand on his arm.

"It's not blind, Tom," she said intently. "But you do have to open your eyes."

With that she walked out of the kitchen while Tom and Calvin exchanged a look that summed up a lifetime of trying to understand and deal with their sister's unswerving faith in God, the Bible, and a special destiny for mankind. It was then that a mischievous light brightened Tom's eyes, and he signaled for his kid brother to come closer so he could whisper in his ear.

A few minutes later Eileen returned from the bathroom to find the kitchen empty. Puzzled, she called out her brothers' names before noticing two piles of clothing, one for each of them, heaped on the kitchen chairs. She shook her head and rolled her eyes. *My two baby brothers really are a couple of overgrown kids*, she thought as she heard the sound of stifled giggling coming from the pantry closet.

Crossing silently to the pantry door, she spoke loudly into the empty room. "Tom?" she cried. "Calvin. What's going on here? Where can they be?" Then with mock horror she let out a shriek. "Oh, my Lord, no! It can't be!"

The giggling grew louder as Eileen carefully and silently propped a chair under the pantry doorknob. A long moment passed before she heard the tentative sounds of the two men, dressed only in their underwear, trying to get out of their hiding place but succeeding only in pushing against the firmly wedged chair.

"Eileen?" Calvin called with alarm. "Eileen? Are you out there? This isn't funny, Eileen."

"Calvin had pizza for dinner, Eileen," pleaded Tom. "Don't leave me in here with him!"

It was Eileen's turn to try to hold back her laughter.

Chapter 3

THE DAY HAD FADED INTO LATE AFTERNOON, the bright sun and singing birds subdued in the deep shadows of encroaching twilight as Tom entered the living room dressed for work in a sport jacket, a pair of comfortable slacks, a button-down shirt, and a simple tie. The badge that bestowed on him the power to enforce and protect hung from a small leather clip on his belt, and he had buttoned his jacket over the shoulder holster so that, even at the close range Calvin was standing, there was no bulge to give away its deadly presence.

"So," Calvin was saying as he finished up the last of a can of beer while a post-football-game analysis droned on the television, "tomorrow night's the biggie, is it?"

Tom grinned. "Want to see how big?" he asked with a twinkle in his eye. With his brother's attention fully at his command he reached into his jacket pocket and produced a small blue jewelry case whose rich velvet sheen suggested something sumptuous and expensive lay inside.

Opening it with a flourish, he produced a dazzling diamond wedding band.

"Wow!" said Calvin, letting out a low whistle. "Not bad. Not bad at all. So," he added slyly, "does this mean you're finally ready to make a commitment?"

Tom gave his brother a playful punch on the shoulder. "Hey, pard," he said. "You know I couldn't afford to give her the ring she deserved when we first got married. And I've been saving up a long, long time for this one." He held it up to the light. "It's a beauty, isn't it?" From the next room he heard Suzie call his name, and quickly returning his prize to his suit jacket pocket, he winked at Calvin and hurried off to answer her summons.

The golden light of dusk spilled across the kitchen as Tom saw his wife of ten years standing in the shadows with her back to him. Sliding silently behind her, he put his arms around her and nuzzled the nape of her neck. It was clear that Tom and Suzie's marriage was as fresh and full of love today as it had been ten years ago.

"Oh," purred Suzie, "there you are. I thought you'd left for work already."

"Without saying good-bye to you?" Tom replied. "Never."

Suzie turned in her husband's arms to face him. "Tom," she whispered in his ear, "I want you to be especially careful out there tonight."

"Why tonight of all nights?" asked Tom.

"Because," she replied, "tomorrow's our special day."

Tom pretended puzzlement. "Tomorrow?" he said,

scratching his head. "What's tomorrow?" Then, snapping his fingers, he feigned inspiration. "Of course!" he said happily. "League bowling night, right?"

Angry and upset, Suzie pulled away from him only to see a broad grin growing on his wide and open face.

"Come on, Sweetheart," he chided. "How could I forget tomorrow? Ten years ago you made me the happiest man on earth."

Her disapproval fading as quickly as it came, Suzie seemed to melt into her husband's arms. "Oh, Tom," she said in a seductive whisper, "it's just that I've been so looking forward to having this time alone."

"Well," said Tom as he returned to his nuzzling, "nobody's going to find us up at Rat Lake. And that's for sure."

Suzie tilted her head to one side to allow her husband to kiss her neck. "That's such a terrible name," she murmured. "Why did anybody name it that in the first place?"

"Probably so no one will go up there" was his muffled reply. After a moment he stopped and looked at her with his characteristic grin. "Pretty good scheme, don't you think?"

"Are you sure you didn't tell a soul about that cottage, Tom?" Suzie insisted.

"No one," promised Tom, holding up three fingers, Scout's honor style.

"Not even Calvin?" Suzie pressed. "It would be just like your brother to show up and pull some kind of juvenile prank."

"Not even Calvin, Honey," Tom reassured her. "It's our

little secret." Then leaning close, he touched her nose with his own. "And speaking of surprises," he added playfully, "I'm going to have a very special surprise waiting for you tomorrow night."

Now it was Suzie's turn to show her childlike side. Squealing with delight, she kissed him again and breathlessly asked, "What? What is it?"

Tom put on the demeanor of a stern adult. "Perhaps," he scolded, "you don't understand the nature of surprises, young lady."

"Oh, please!" she begged. "Please, please, please tell me!" But instead Tom silenced her pleas with another kiss.

At that moment Calvin walked in. "Okay, okay," he crowed, "break it up, you two. This isn't high school, for crying out loud!"

Tom and Suzie ignored him and deliberately exchanged one long, last kiss. "See you in the morning," he said when at last they came up for air.

"Good night, Sweetheart," Suzie cooed. "And please . . . be careful."

Tom stroked her face and turned to Calvin. "C'mon, you little weasel," he said. "You're parked behind me."

As they left, walking out the front door and down to the driveway, the last rays of daylight faded. Unnoticed by either brother was the soft wavering glow of a television, leaking light from the ground-level window that opened onto Jason's bedroom.

In the subterranean reaches of his musty, messy lair Jason sat on an unmade bed, mesmerized by the ghostly light of the screen, watching with rapt attention as a man spoke directly into the camera, his eyes alight with a strange and unearthly fire, his soft voice so compelling it seemed to be coming from inside Jason himself. A small ponytail hung below the collar of his immaculately tailored suit, and his thick dark hair was slicked back off his bony forehead. The face radiated power, confidence, and an all-encompassing wisdom that seemed to reach through the camera in a personal appeal to each of his millions upon millions of viewers. FRANCO MACALOUSSO, read the superimposed caption beneath the desk where he sat: PRESIDENT OF THE EUROPEAN UNITY PROJECT.

"The real goal," Macalousso was saying in a voice as smooth as silk and as rich as platinum, "is the realization of the true potential that lies within us all. There is an enormous power that lies slumbering within each of us. My friends, if we will but open our minds, one and all at the same time with the same purpose, then whatever it is that we believe together will become a reality."

Even as Jason watched and listened, he could feel his fingers begin to tremble where they rested lightly on the Ouija board he had laid out before him. Slowly, eerily, the pointer began to move, inching across the letters and symbols, slowly spelling out its message.

"Citizens of the world," Macalousso continued, stretching his arms wide, "unity is the key that can unlock the door to the wondrous potential within each of us. Black, white; male, female . . . it doesn't matter." He touched his long and perfectly manicured finger to his forehead. "The power of our minds unites us. And the strength of our unity empowers us."

While he spoke, the pointer under Jason's fingers made its slow but relentless circuit around the board. As the potent television prophet concluded his heartfelt address, Jason looked down at the last letter. It was an *M*. He quickly added it to the others he had scrawled on a scrap of paper. Together they spelled out a message Jason was not sure he understood. Nor was he sure why the sight of those two simple words sent a cold chill down his spine. For a long moment he looked at the paper in his trembling hands. Then slowly, deliberately, he whispered aloud what was written there.

"I AM."

Setting down the scrap and reaching out to turn off the television, Jason stretched out on his bed, his hands behind his head. He had a lot to think about tonight. A lot to ponder. Franco Macalousso and the monkeys on the island. Sandy bananas and I AM. What did it all mean?

Yet even as Jason struggled with such questions, drifting into a fevered and dream-haunted sleep, some people had gathered—on a street in his own hometown, in the penthouse suite of a building he passed by every day—who already knew the answers. They were men who had paid dearly to possess such knowledge, men who served a master who had unlocked for them power and pleasure beyond their wildest imaginings.

To call them men was only a half-truth. Even the confused mind of Jason would know that a man is more than just a body in a familiar shape; more than a head and face, hands and feet. The essence of man lay deeper inside in an invisible realm that could be seen only with special eyes that could look within. What defined a man, in short, was his spirit, and for this sinister group of five, dressed in black and gathered around a candlelit table, a soul was something that each had bargained away a long time ago.

In the dark room, made darker by the shadows of candles held in sconces along the walls, the men stood, four of them, flanked two on each side, facing toward a fifth, who addressed them from the head of the long table and was clearly in command of the gathering. The man's totally bald head gleamed in the dim light, an earring glinting in one earlobe, a long black robe reaching down his legs, which were sheathed in spit-polished knee-high black boots. His name was Zack Probert, and in his hands he held a strange, twisted object that the others looked upon with a mixture of fear and fascination.

In the center of the table around which they had congregated was a large, half-finished model of a tower. Alongside it was one of the two pieces that would complete the replica. Zack Probert held the other piece.

Staring up through the ceiling into the very vault of heaven itself, Probert began to speak, his voice as loud and booming as a thunderclap and just as ominous. "He cast us from heaven," he intoned, "but it was only the battle He won. The war is still being waged. And now our powers grow." He looked around at the others. "Feel them growing within you! When the final conflict commences, we will win this time . . . win because we will unite the power of our creation against His."

Around the table the other men, also attired in black robes, murmured their agreement. Although they had names—Morgan Scott, Carl Sweig, Sam Record, and Victor Morin—they had long ago given up their individual identities, merging their lives and purposes to the grand designs of the infernal conspiracy even now unfolding. Perhaps they had once been men. Perhaps they had once been angels. All that was certain on that ordinary evening in that ordinary town was that, once these creatures had been loosed, nothing would ever be ordinary again.

As one of his minions picked up the tower piece from the table and put it in its place, Zack Probert looked up once again to thunder at the very throne of heaven. "You're going to run away again, aren't You?" he sneered. "You did it once before, at this very tower." Lifting the final piece high in his arms, Probert carefully set it in place, completing the miniature image of a huge and complex structure— a structure once designed to reach up into God's kingdom itself—the Tower of Babel.

The final part locked in, Probert stepped back to regard his handiwork, turning to his associates and pointing at the creation before them. "Once again the mystery of Babel will be revealed for all to see and pay homage! Your very creation will unite as one . . . against its own Creator! And it is for this glorious day that we must now prepare."

Turning to the figure nearest him, the one known by the earthly name of Morgan Scott, Probert intoned with the sickly delight of pure evil, "And who will give us a peek into the other side tonight?"

Scott turned to his superior and straightened as if at attention. "His name," he reported, "is Tim Tucker. He's a perfect candidate for our test, especially since he teaches a course in psychic phenomena. Here is a man whose mind is already wide open to receive us."

"Yes," said Probert, stroking the close-cropped beard on his chin. "Just as they all will soon be."

The acolytes around him closed their eyes and bowed their heads, taking their cue from Probert. As if with one mind and one will, they reached out beyond the dark confines of their secret hiding place, out into the night, seeking and searching for their chosen victim.

Across town, along a leafy boulevard of apartment buildings not far from the university campus, a lone light shone from the fourteenth floor of a particularly imposing edifice. It was to this very destination that Probert and his apprentices directed their malevolent energies, through the thin glass and into the bedroom of Tim and Diane Tucker.

A couple in their early thirties, the Tuckers were lying in bed, getting ready to call it a night after a long and active day. Tim had already begun to doze, and Diane, careful not to disturb her hardworking husband, softly turned the pages of the Bible she was perusing.

Suddenly, as though prompted by a will not his own, Tim's eyes popped open, and he sat bolt upright in bed. In a matter of seconds he had gone from complete relaxation on the verge of deep sleep to a state of intense agitation, every muscle in his body straining and sweat popping from the pores of his scalp. Looking over at his wife as if finding a stranger in bed next to him, his eyes fell upon the Bible laying open on her lap.

"Tim," his wife said, frightened and startled by the remarkable transformation he had undergone, "are you all right? What's the matter?"

His wild eyes went from his wife's horror-stricken face to the Bible. He pointed at it, snatched it from her, and hurled it into the glass door of an entertainment unit across the room.

"Tim!" his wife screamed, leaping from the bed. "What are you doing? Stop it! You're scaring me!"

Now transformed into something as close to a wild animal as a human being could become, Tim clutched at his skull as if the brain inside had swollen and was trying to break through the solid bone. Pure rage contorted his face, and he gestured at the Bible lying in the shards of broken glass.

"There's no room in this world for lies like those!" he snarled, then fixed her with an expression of incomprehensible malice. "You just don't get it, do you?" he hissed. "It's people like you who are holding all the rest of us back. It's because of your kind that we can't bring the world together. You and your kind are standing in the way, thinking that you are the only ones who know the truth!"

With catlike stealth he bounded from the bed and took a menacing step toward her.

"Tim!" screamed the terrified Diane.

Flipping over a night table, Tim sent a lamp crashing into the wall and moved quickly to block Diane's escape through the bedroom door.

"The time has come to free the world of haters," Tim announced ominously.

"The haters? What haters?" Diane asked between sobs. "What are you talking about?"

"As if you didn't know," Tim sneered, showing his teeth like an animal ready to pounce. "Well, let me clue you in. You're going to die. All of you are going to die!"

Diane's scream pierced the night as she vainly tried to elude her advancing husband. With a lightning-quick strike, he reached out and grabbed her by the hair, pulling her to the floor and standing over her, for all the world like a beast about to deliver the deathblow to its next meal.

Tom was less than a block away when his radio crackled to life with an emergency response request for a domestic disturbance.

"Attention, all units," the dispatcher broadcast, "we have reports of a domestic situation at 63 Nelson. Car 21, please report your location."

Tom had grabbed the handset almost before the dispatcher was finished. "This is Detective Canboro. I'm coming up on the scene now. Show me that domestic."

As he hit the switch on the siren, a voice from the radio on the dash cut through the static. "Ten four, Detective," the dispatcher confirmed. "Car 21 will back you up."

Arriving at the apartment block, Tom moved from

the car, through the lobby, and to the elevator in one unbroken action, bringing years of experience and professionalism to what could be a potentially dangerous situation. As he stepped out of the elevator and strode down the hall toward the door from which screams and crashing furniture could be heard, he reminded himself once again that it was as easy for a cop to get killed trying to break up a fight between warring spouses as it was in a full-scale crack house shoot-up. But from the sounds of the terrified shrieking he heard, he also knew he couldn't afford to be too cautious. Someone needed his help—and needed it badly.

"Police!" he shouted, banging on the door. "Open up!" When he heard only more screams and the sounds of splintering furniture, he knew he had to make his move. Throwing all of his hefty frame against the door, he easily snapped the deadbolt from its anchor and, propelled by the momentum, charged into the apartment. "Police!" he shouted again, making sure whoever it was knew exactly who he was.

Making an instant appraisal of the layout of the apartment, Tom saw thrashing shadows coming from a room down the hall. In a few swift steps he made his way to the dining room entrance. "Freeze!" he shouted even before he was able to fully take in the scene of utter chaos and terror before him.

Diane, cowering in a corner, was still being held by her hair in the hands of her crazed husband. Several welts had begun to appear on her face and shoulders where he had rained down blows on her. Pulling out his gun in one seamless motion, Tom leveled it directly at Tim's face.

"Police," he repeated. "Hold it right there, pal."

With barely a glance in his direction, Tim returned to his brutal task. Raising his hand to deliver another stinging slap, he stopped only when Tom, louder this time, repeated, "I said, 'Hold it.'" To underscore his determination, he moved a step closer and, reaching up, grabbed the crazed man by his wrist.

Just as he was trying to wrench free, Tim noticed the service revolver pointed at him in the officer's other hand. For a moment, sanity seemed to return as he let his wife drop and turned to fully confront Tom.

"I'm afraid it's a little too late for heroics, Officer," he said in a curiously flat, uninflected monotone. "You see, the battle has only just begun." He held up his finger as if delivering a closing argument in court. "And make no mistake about it. Franco Macalousso will prevail. Together we will beat Him this time."

Tom knew better than to engage a suspect in conversation before he was safely in custody, but something about the mention of Macalousso prompted him to ask the inevitable question.

"Who?" he queried. "Beat who?"

Tim grinned an evil, mirthless smile. "Why," he replied as if delivering the morning weather report, "God, of course."

Tom shook his head. Maybe it was a full moon or something, but there was no question about it—the nuts were really out tonight. "Okay," he said grimly. "Maybe you and your buddies are going to beat God, but for right now I suggest you get your hands behind your back. You're under arrest."

Tim's grin got wider. He made a move as if to oblige, bringing his hands around to the small of his back, but then in a sequence of actions so strange and inexplicable that, even later, Tom had trouble crediting what his eyes had seen, the tables were turned.

In the literal blink of an eye, Tom noticed his suspect glancing over at a large carving knife resting on a sideboard. *It's halfway across the room,* he would remember telling himself. *There's no way*—

In the next second, what was impossible became only too real as the knife somehow appeared in Tim's waiting hand. Had he moved at lightning speed across the room to grab it? Had he exercised some uncanny power of mind over matter to bring it to him? Tom didn't know and, for the moment, didn't have the luxury of asking questions. Before Tom's astonished eyes, Tim grabbed Diane, pulled her to her feet, and held the knife tightly against her pulsating throat.

"As I said, Officer," Tim croaked, "you're just a little too late to save the day. The war on the haters has already commenced. Nothing, not even your precious almighty God in heaven, can stop us now."

Later, when Tom replayed the incident in his mind, he couldn't shake the uneasy feeling that even as the obviously deranged suspect was saying the words, they were not his own—that somebody or something had put them in Tim's mouth and forced him to speak them. It was a deep and gravelly voice that seemed to fill the room. Although Tim's lips moved, Tom could almost swear he could hear the words echoing in his own head, coming through empty space into that room from across a distant gulf.

In reality, the gulf was only that between the tense scene unfolding and the hidden headquarters of Zack Probert and the team he had assembled around him. Still standing in intense concentration around the table on which rested the elaborate model of Babel's tower, the one called Sam Record looked up from under his cowl and said simply, "It's time, sir."

"Excellent," replied Zack without opening his eyes. "Then let's terminate, gentlemen." Turning to the one called Morgan, the lids of his large black eyes slowly rising, he posed a one-word question. "Floor?" he asked.

"Fourteen, sir," was the reply.

"Excellent," Probert breathed. "That should certainly do the trick." And at his unspoken command, the four men around him closed their eyes and lowered their heads for one last, deadly burst of pure concentrated mental energy.

That energy shot at the speed of light across town and into the overheated mind of Tim Tucker. Still standing in front of Tom, the razor-sharp blade of the carving knife pressed to Diane's throat, he spoke clearly and firmly.

"Let's have the gun," he commanded. When Tom hesitated, Tim pushed the knife a little closer to his wife's pulsing jugular vein.

Tom's well-trained mind was also in overdrive. The last

thing he wanted to do was to hand over his weapon to a maniac. But what was his alternative?

"Maybe we should talk about this," he ventured.

"The gun!" Tim demanded. "Now!" His wife whimpered at the sound of his bellowing voice.

As reluctant as he was to admit it, Tom could see no other way out of this life-threatening impasse. Emptying the chamber, he lowered his weapon and set it on the dining room table.

"Okay, partner," he said in his most soothing voice, "let's just all take it easy. The main thing is, no one gets hurt. Why don't you just let the little lady there go?"

Tim's face went through contortions of loathing and hatred. "Don't patronize me," he snarled. "I've already told you. We're in control. There is nothing anyone can do to stop us—"

Then as suddenly as the frenzy had come over him, it seemed to subside. A look of peace and calm washed over his face as he dropped the knife and let his wife go.

Sobbing uncontrollably, Diane staggered over to Tom and hid behind him. Kicking the knife out of reach across the floor, he quickly retrieved his revolver and dropped in a Speedloader that he kept in a case on his belt.

Tim hardly seemed to notice. His attention had been drawn to a large picture window that overlooked the city nightscape from the apartment's fourteenth-floor vantage-point. Tom followed his gaze, but could not see what had so fascinated his suspect. A strange smile suffusing his face, Tim moved slowly, deliberately, toward the window.

"Hold it right there, mister," Tom barked, raising the gun again.

Just as Tim had foreseen, it was too late to stop what had already been put in motion. From a slow walk, he began taking long strides and then broke into a full-tilt run, straight toward his own ghostly reflection.

"Stop!" Tom shouted. "We're—"

His words were cut short by a horrendous sound of shattering glass as Tim hit the window at full velocity and crashed through, his arms and legs flailing in midair before he began his sickening plunge to the ground below. Diane's fresh screams echoed in Tom's ears as he rushed to the gaping hole in the window through which a cold night wind now blew.

There below he could see the crumpled body of Tim Tucker lying spread-eagle, his limbs twisted in grotesque parody of human form, on the hood of a car. He could hear the distant sounds of sirens and honking horns, and somewhere from one of the nearby apartments, a man shouting and a woman screaming.

"—fourteen floors up," Tom said, completing what he had begun what seemed like a heartbeat ago.

Chapter 4

IT HAD BEEN A NIGHT OF HORROR for Tom Canboro, the ultimate nightmare of every dedicated police officer, unable to stop a spiral of violence, unable to prevent the senseless death of another citizen. Although his numbed brain could hardly wrap itself around the events that had transpired in the Tucker apartment, he was sure of two things: one man was dead and one woman was left a widow.

But Tom's evening had only just begun, and the terror was spreading, reaching its tentacles far into the sleeping streets of the city and its suburbs. When it struck again, it would be much closer to the life that he had built for himself, much closer to the people he most loved and cared for.

Even as Tom hurried down the hallway toward the terrible circumstances of Tim Tucker's last night on earth, back at his own home, uncannily similar events were playing themselves out. The eerie coincidences began unfolding sometime after he left for work, departing with Calvin, who drove back to his own place. Dusk had turned to deepest night when Suzie, sitting at her home office desk going over details for an upcoming show and making notes for her partner, Helen Hannah, heard strange moans and shouts coming from Jason's lair in the basement. A palpable sense of dread followed her through the hallway and down the dark flight of stairs where she found Jason cowering in a corner, the Ouija board clutched in his white-knuckled hand. The words spewing from his mouth were hardly intelligible, but she was able to make out the name Franco Macalousso and the word *haters* repeated again and again.

"Jason!" she shouted, wondering now whether Tom hadn't been right after all. Maybe a home or a hospital was the best place for her troubled brother. "What's the matter? What are you talking about?"

But Jason seemed far away, lost in a dark and frightful world of his own. "Haters," he mumbled. "Must stop the haters. Macalousso has commanded . . . kill the haters."

"What haters?" Suzie urgently queried. "Jason, snap out of it! It's your sister . . . Suzie."

At the sound of her name, Jason seemed to come out of his trance. Looking at her as if noticing her presence for the first time, he stood up, gesturing angrily with the Ouija board still in his hand. "Where's Eileen?" he demanded. Seeing his sister's blank look, he shouted even louder. "Don't pretend you don't know! I can see your hand! I can see the sign! I'm not stupid!"

Suzie looked down at her hand. There was nothing to see but the same familiar fingers, palm, and polished nails. "What's the matter with my hand?" she asked, her voice trembling with alarm. "Jason, what are you talking about? You're scaring me."

With a wordless cry he pushed past her and bounded up the stairs, still clutching the Ouija board as if it were a life preserver on a sinking ship. "Jason!" Suzie called after him and rushed to follow his retreating shadow.

None of the players in the twin tragedies could have known that the events in the Canboro home and those across town at the Tucker apartment were unfolding at precisely the same time, as though in mirror image of each other. Even as Tom found the door that opened into Tim and Diane's foyer, Suzie put her hand to the knob that opened into a bedroom where Jason crouched in a dark corner. Even as Tom pleaded with the crazed husband to listen to reason, Suzie was trying to convince her frantic brother to do the same. Finally, even as Tom watched helplessly as Tim Tucker plunged to his death from a fourteenth-story window, Suzie screamed in horror as Jason leaped suddenly to his feet and jumped headfirst through the plate glass of the first-floor window and onto the asphalt driveway below.

Suzie, knocked to the floor in Jason's suicidal rush, stumbled to her feet. Hoping against hope that her brother would somehow have survived his plunge out the window, she rushed out the front door. She found him still lying on the ground, covered with shattered glass. The Ouija board lay where it had fallen from his hand. Her heart stopped for a breathless moment as she approached, looking for some—for any—sign of life. At the same moment when Tom was trying his best to comfort the bereaved Diane Tucker, Suzie saw her brother stir and feebly try to rise to his feet.

"Jason!" she cried as she hurried to his side. "Thank God, you're all right!"

Her brother, possessed now by some seemingly supernatural source of power, brushed her aside and stood, blood streaming down his face from a deep gash in his scalp, staring at her as if seeing some specter materializing from the night.

"Jason," Suzie continued with all the calmness she could muster. "Calm down. Don't worry. It's just me . . . Suzie. Your sister." From across the street, a neighbor's upstairs light went on and Suzie found herself desperately hoping that she could get her brother back into the house before anyone else became involved. "Everything's going to be all right," she continued, trying her best to make it sound true.

"No, it's not," shot back Jason, a terrible fear tearing at his voice. "You don't understand." He was searching the sky as he had done earlier that day, looking for something Suzie could only guess at. "They've found me, don't you see?" he mumbled, gazing at the stars as though they were eyes staring down at him. "But it wasn't supposed to be like this. I knew they were out there . . . that I could contact them . . . but they weren't supposed to be so"—he stopped, choking on the word—"evil."

"Who, Jason?" Suzie pressed. "Who found you? Who's evil?"

In answer, Jason could only point to the sky. "They are," he intoned solemnly, then shook his head as if he couldn't believe the words that were coming from his mouth. "They . . . they wanted to kill . . . Eileen!"

"Who did?" Suzie repeated. She couldn't even begin to make sense of what he was telling her, and her mind was going in frantic circles trying to think of what to do next for Jason and for his safety. "Who would want to—"

She was interrupted by the arrival of Mike, the good-natured next-door neighbor who had been awakened by the crashing of glass and the frightened voice coming from the Canboros' driveway.

"Sue?" he was saying as he emerged from around the garage. "What's going on? Is everything okay?" It was then that he noticed Jason's bloodstained face and clothing. "Jason!" he said, shocked and alarmed. "What the heck happened to—"

The abject terror in Jason's eyes stopped him dead in his tracks. "Hey," he said, holding up his hands. "It's going to be all right, buddy. It's just me, Mike. From next door."

His words seemed to vanish in the dark abyss that had opened up between Jason's ears. The presence of his neighbor and his sister seemed to fade from his consciousness as his gaze returned to the stars in the night sky above. "I would have done it," he said, shocked at the revelation that was dawning on him. "I would have killed her if she had been here." He sobbed. "God help me, I would have."

'Killed'?" Mike echoed. "What are you talking about there, Jason?" He turned to Suzie. "I better call the cops."

"No!" Suzie said a little too insistently, then tried to calm herself. "We . . . don't need the cops in on this. He'll be fine. He's, you know, just a little upset. Please, let's keep this to ourselves, Mike."

The neighbor shook his head adamantly. "Sorry, Suze," he said. "When he starts talking about killing someone . . . well, I think it's better if we let the proper authorities handle the situation."

"But—" Suzie began, then stopped. Mike had already turned and was hurrying back to his house, where his wife was waiting in the front door.

As events unfolded on the once quiet street of the Canboros' neighborhood, Tom was completing the grim task of wrapping up the crime scene at the Tucker suicide site. The flashing red police lights lit the street with a lurid glow as paramedics loaded the coroner's wagon with the body bag and Tom completed the last sheet in what seemed an endless pile of official paperwork.

From one of the many squad cars at the scene, he noticed a familiar face emerging. It was Kenny Rice, who had worked side by side with Tom as his partner since they were both rookie detectives. Gesturing the officer over, he took him aside and tried to piece together for him what had just happened. *Maybe*, he thought, *if I tell it to someone else, it will make more sense to me.*

"It was incredible, Kenny," Tom was saying. "I mean,

that knife must have been twenty feet away from us if it was an inch. There's simply no way he could have reached it. So—picture it—there I am, standing helplessly by, thinking this guy is about to slice his wife wide open, when, out of nowhere, he just . . . stops." Tom swallowed hard as he relived the traumatic sequence of events. No matter how many times he saw it in the line of duty, he could just never get used to watching a man die.

"Next thing I know," he continued, steeling himself once again, "it was like he snapped or something. He just took a dive through that window like an Olympic champion doing a half gainer." He shook his head. "I don't know," he concluded. "It just doesn't make any sense. I can't put it together."

Kenny listened carefully, knowing that this seasoned officer was trying to relieve some of the burden of his job. Shaking his head, he rested a hand on Tom's shoulder. "I don't know if this helps," he ventured, "but according to his wife, this Tucker guy was doing a lot of dabbling in the occult lately. Apparently he taught a course on witchcraft and magic up at the college. Under those circumstances, who knows what we might be dealing with here."

Tom smiled and reached over to touch the gold cross hanging around the policeman's neck. "I'll tell you one thing, partner," he said, and was surprised that he more than half believed what he was about to say. "If this was the devil's handiwork, then I wish it had been you up there instead of me."

Another uniformed officer hurried up to Tom. "Detective Canboro," she said, "seems we've got another ten fifty-two in progress. Domestic disturbance."

Tom groaned. "I've had enough for tonight," he protested. "Can't you put someone else on it?"

The officer fixed him with a deadly serious look. "I would, Tom," she said. "You know that. Except this one's coming from your address."

Tom blanched, then exchanged a quick look with Kenny. More than once he had confided in his friend and fellow officer about his troubled brother-in-law. "Jason," he whispered.

Nodding knowingly, Kenny slapped him on the back. "You better get over there, partner," he said. "I'll cover for you around here."

"I owe you one," replied Tom. With a quick squeeze of Kenny's forearm he hurried off to his waiting car. As he crossed the crowded street, he glanced into the shadows of an alleyway where a figure lurked. The two locked eyes, and when Zack Probert stepped into the halo of a street lamp, Tom felt a chill run through his body. There was something about the strange figure, a palpable sense of dread that he seemed to carry with him. With his gleaming bald head, earring, and black jackboots, he could have passed for any number of stranger denizens of the city. But something else about the stranger—the way his cold, reptilian eyes followed Tom across the street—lodged in the back of the detective's skull like a premonition of bad tidings.

Sliding into the driver's seat, Tom punched the siren button and went screaming off into the darkness, trailed by that same pair of eyes, that same sinister appraisal, as if the man were an undertaker sizing up a customer for a custom-fitted coffin.

Sirens blazing, running red lights and weaving around late night traffic, Tom arrived at his home in record time. A securely restrained Jason was just being trundled off into the back of an ambulance. In a blink of an eye, he summed up the situation—noticing his next-door neighbor, Mike, giving an animated report to an attending officer and seeing Suzie trying to pick up the shards of glass off the driveway. Barely taking time to turn off the ignition, Tom leaped from the car and hurried across the lawn to his wife.

The look of dull despair in Suzie's eyes lifted the moment she saw her husband approaching, and she fell into his waiting arms, finally allowing herself the freedom to cry. It had been a harrowing night. More than anything, she needed the comfort and security of his strong embrace. Tenderly, as only a loving husband can, he waited until her sobs subsided. He didn't need words to explain what the look she gave next meant. She needed to be close to her brother, in case she might somehow be able to help him out of the dark pit into which he had fallen. With his arm around her shoulders, Tom led her to his car and followed the ambulance to the hospital.

Suzie was able to pull herself together enough to give her husband a coherent account of what had happened. "Eileen had left," she was saying, "and I was doing some work in my office. All of a sudden, I heard Jason starting to scream." She shuddered. "It was terrible, Tom." She took a deep breath to steady herself. "Anyway," she continued after a moment, "when I got to his room, he was ranting and raving and yelling like he was going absolutely—" She stopped, catching herself before she uttered the forbidden word, as Tom shot her a knowing glance. "Let's just say he was very upset," she concluded.

Tom nodded. "Well," he said after a moment, "whatever it was that got into your brother, at least he's going someplace where they can really help him." He gestured to the ambulance lights ahead of them on the road.

Suzie shook her head. She needed to make him understand. "It was different this time, Tom. It wasn't just his usual . . . attitude."

Tom caught the utter seriousness of her tone and turned to look at her. There, in her eyes, he could see the truth of what she was saying. "What exactly do you mean, Suze?"

She sat forward in her seat, gratified that she had at last captured her husband's full attention. "It's hard to explain," she admitted. "It was like he wasn't just making up stories in his head. He really believed what he was saying. Really and truly believed every word. It was almost like . . . he was someone else."

Tom couldn't resist a gentle gibe. "Do you think the aliens finally got him?" he asked with a straight face.

She gave him a reproachful look, refusing to acknowledge his grin. "This isn't funny, Tom," she retorted. "I'm really scared, okay? I think it might be very serious this time. Not aliens. Not monkeys. Something else. Something that gives me the creeps."

To underline her point, she reached into her handbag and produced the two halves of the Ouija board, snapped in half from Jason's tumble out the window. "He was playing with this," she said.

In the car's semidarkness, Tom squinted at the strange device with its arcane symbols and letters. "Wow," he said. "I haven't seen one of those things since I was a kid." He nodded in acknowledgment. "So . . . maybe it wasn't the aliens." But unable to leave well enough alone, he couldn't help adding, "Maybe it was Elvis."

The look Suzie gave him this time was enough to convince Tom that the joking was over for good. "I'm trying to be serious," his wife pleaded. "I've heard things about these boards. Spooky things. I'm afraid he might have been—"

Tom cut her off with an impatient gesture. "No, no, no," he insisted. "Don't even think about going there, Sweetheart. This isn't one of your TV shows. We're not looking for the most dramatic explanation we can find. There's a reason for all of this. And it's right in the here and now." But even as he spoke the words, he wondered if she was really listening. After all, he had tried out this argument a hundred times before, and it never did any good. Except that maybe this time, things *were* different.

He took a deep breath and plunged ahead. "Your brother is mentally ill, Honey. These things happen. It's not his fault. It's not anyone's fault. You have to try and learn just to accept that."

Suzie shook her head vehemently. "No, Tom," she insisted. "This time it was different. He wasn't himself. You may be sure he's out of his mind, and it's your right to think whatever you want. But let me ask you something. Do you think I'm sane?"

"Of course I do," Tom replied. "What kind of a—"

"Then please don't dismiss what I'm telling you," Suzie interjected.

"I'm not dismissing it," Tom responded. "I'm just saying I don't know how clearly you're seeing the big picture, that's all. I mean, he is your brother, Suzie."

"You haven't been listening to a word I've been saying," his wife accused him.

Tom sighed. A long moment passed. "All right," he finally said. "I'm sorry. Just tell me again . . . what happened?"

Suzie took a deep breath, gathering up her strength. She had to get through to this thickheaded man. "It was just the way he was yelling," she said. "The words he was saying. It was like they weren't coming from his body. He kept talking about that Franco Macalousso character from television. You know, the European Unity guy. And one thing he kept saying over and over was that we had to stop the haters. I'm not sure exactly who the haters are, but it seemed a matter of life and death to—" Her voice trailed off as she saw the look that had come over her husband's transfixed face. "What, Tom?" she asked. "What is it?"

"What else did he say?" Tom pressed in a low, firm voice. Before she could answer, the ambulance pulled into the emergency entrance of the hospital, and the paramedics jumped out to deliver their cargo.

Chapter 5

THE FACES OF TOM AND SUZIE CANBORO looked pale and wan under the harsh fluorescent lights of the hospital corridor. There, outside the waiting room, they spent their anxious minutes in the company of others who hoped and prayed for a doctor or nurse to deliver good news about their friends or loved ones. Somewhere in the back of everyone's mind was the knowledge that one day, even a day like this one, it might be him or her in the hospital room hooked up to wires and tubes as life drained away and preparation was made at last to face the reality of what was waiting on the other side—heaven or hell, God or the devil. It was a choice each had made long ago. And it was only a matter of time before each person reaped the consequences of that decision.

Tonight, they hoped, would not be that time. Tonight was for good wishes and fervent prayer, for positive thinking and putting on a brave front. As Tom and Suzie waited with the others to hear what their doctors could tell them about Jason, they engaged in a fiercely whispered conversation, struggling to make sense of the story they had managed to piece together that would explain the bizarre events of the evening.

"Well, how else are you going to explain it?" Suzie demanded of her husband. "Two guys who are complete strangers to each other, on opposite sides of the city, suddenly and at the same time going completely nuts, talking about the same thing and then, for no reason anyone can tell, both jumping out the window? I'd sure like to hear you explain that one away, Tom."

At that moment a nurse approached and, gesturing for them to follow her, led Tom and Suzie through the maze of corridors to a hospital room in the psychiatric ward where a doctor waited for them. On the other side of the door they could hear shouts and screams of an only too familiar voice: Jason's.

"Mrs. Canboro," said the doctor, a pleasant-faced young man in a white coat with a pocket full of pens, holding a clipboard in one hand. "We'd like to have a word with you about your brother." Turning to Tom, he saw the badge clipped to the detective's belt. "Officer," he said, "if you don't mind . . ."

"That's okay," replied Tom. "I'm her husband. Shoot, Doc."

The doctor cleared his throat, trying to be heard over the bloodcurdling shouts from the other room. "We've given Jason something to help calm him down," the physician said. "We're . . . waiting for it to take effect. But even if we get him stabilized, he's going to need a complete examination. Top to bottom. We'd like to start with one of our staff psychiatrists having a little talk with him in the morning."

From the other room Jason's terrified shrieking got even louder. Unable to stand hearing her brother's anguish another moment, Suzie brushed past the doctor and pushed open the door.

Lying on a hospital bed and strapped down by his arms and legs, Jason thrashed and squirmed like a landed fish. His eyes grew large when he saw his sister and brother-in-law, and he raised his head off the pillow to get a better view.

"Suzie?" he shouted. "Thank God, you're here! Whatever you do, Suze, don't let them keep me here. We don't know who they are, who they're pretending to be. And we can't take any chances!"

Suzie turned to the doctor, who could only shrug and raise his eyebrows.

"Does he really have to stay here tonight?" she asked. "What if we were to bring him back in the morning? You could do your tests then."

"Yeah," echoed the wild-eyed Jason. "That's right. We'll be back in the morning. Just don't leave me here tonight!"

The doctor shook his head, firm in his resolve. "I'm afraid that's not possible, Mrs. Canboro," he replied. "Your brother jumped out of a window. That's an attempted suicide, and that makes him a danger to himself. The law clearly states that we have to keep him here for observation for at least twenty-four hours."

Suzie heaved an exasperated sigh. "But what if I sign a release or something that would relieve you of any—"

"I'm sorry," said the doctor, cutting her off curtly. "It's simply out of my hands."

"No! No!" shouted Jason, straining at the straps that held him.

Her heart about to break at the mere sight of his suffering, Suzie turned to Tom. "I'm going to try to talk to him," she said, and her husband nodded sympathetically. That was one reason he loved his wife so much—she was loyal, even to a fault.

"You know," he said with a smile, "for a guy who is so afraid that Big Brother is always watching him, I'd say Jason is pretty lucky to have a big sister around."

Backing out of the room with the doctor, Tom returned to the waiting room where he poured a cup of coffee from a pot on a hot plate. Almost gagging on the day-old brew, he set the cup back down just in time to see his own sister, Eileen, rushing down the hall.

"I came as soon as I heard," Eileen said, genuine concern written on her kindly features. "Is Jason going to be all right, Tom?"

"I hope so," Tom responded. "But to be honest, Eileen, nothing's going to happen until someone can reach into that head of his and tighten up a few of those loose screws."

Eileen put her hand on her brother's arm. "I'd like to talk to him," she said. "I think maybe I can help."

Tom angrily pulled away and raised his hand as if he were commanding an onrushing car to slam on its brakes. "Hold it right there," he told Eileen. "We're only too aware of what you have to offer him, Eileen, and you can take it from me . . . that's exactly what he doesn't need right now."

The expression that came over Eileen's face summed up exactly the anger she felt toward Tom's stubbornness as well as the sadness that came from being misunderstood and underestimated for so long.

"Look, Eileen," he said, softening a bit at the pain he could see etched on her features. "I know all this religion stuff is important to you, and I wouldn't ever want to take away whatever comfort it brings into your life." He sighed. This was another conversation he'd had one too many times. "But you've got to understand, Sis. It's just not the answer to everything. Jason is facing some very serious problems right now. Mental and emotional problems. He needs a competent doctor. Not a faith-healing preacher."

"How would you know what he needs?" shot back Eileen. "You've never even bothered to take the time to listen to what he has to say."

Tom snorted derisively. "Don't give me that," he replied. "As far as I'm concerned if the first words of any sentence have anything to do with the subject of UFOs, psychic phenomena, or Jesus Christ, that's all I need to hear. He can stop right there. I know what's coming after that, and I'm not interested."

"That's because you've got a bad habit of never letting anyone finish a sentence" was Eileen's spirited response. She always had been more than a match for either one of her brothers. "Maybe if you did, just for once, you might actually learn something, Tom. Something that might get past that thick hide and change your—"

"What?" Tom interrupted. "Change my what, Eileen? My mind? My life? Is that what you're trying to say? Why don't you open your ears and listen to what's coming out of your own mouth for once? You might be surprised to hear some of the garbage that you're trying to pass off as the truth and get people to believe."

Eileen took a deep breath in preparation for letting her kid brother get what was coming to him. But she stopped, looking around. This was family business, and no one needed to hear them hanging out their dirty laundry. "Listen, Tom," she said, biting down hard on her anger and resentment, "just because you don't believe in God, that doesn't mean—"

"Hold on a second there," Tom interrupted again. "I never said I didn't believe in God."

"Well"—Eileen stuck out her chin in an unmistakable challenge—"do you?"

Tom paused a long moment. Then another. "Look," he said at last, "that's a very complicated question, and I don't have time to—"

"There's nothing complicated about it," was Eileen's feisty rejoinder. "Either you do, or you don't." She squinted one eye and looked at him hard. "When was the last time you cracked open the Bible, Brother?"

"I don't need to open the Bible to believe in God," Tom shot back, bristling at his sister's boldness. "That's your whole problem, Eileen. You think all that stuff is real. That it all happened and all those predictions are going to come true. Well, I've got news for you. It ain't. None of it. Not one bit."

"That's where you're wrong, Tom," Eileen countered with calm assurance. "It is real. Every last word. Every dotted *i* and every crossed *t*."

"Like Noah's ark?" Tom spat back disdainfully. "Like Jonah in the belly of a flippin' whale? Come on, Eileen. You really expect me to swallow, pardon the pun, some story about a guy living for a week in a whale's smelly guts? Get a grip on reality here, girl. It's a storybook. Legends and myths. Not history. Not science."

It was a standoff. As close and caring as they were as brother and sister, there were issues of life and death over which they had never been able to see eye to eye. Tom felt sad and angry all over again. He wished he could do something, anything, to make his sister feel better. But pretending to believe all that nonsense she was always spouting from the Bible was going too far. It wouldn't be fair to him or to her.

"Look," he said wearily. "I'll tell you what I'm going to do." He held up his hands. "Let's let this drop for right now. We'll both pretend we didn't have this conversation one more time. Then, come next Sunday, you and I will go to that church of yours together."

Eileen's face softened at his words, a look of delight replacing the frustration that had been written there a moment before. "Really?" she said. "Do you promise?"

"Scout's honor," Tom replied, holding up two fingers. "Now, you get on that heavenly horn of yours and tell the Big Guy upstairs that I'll be there, standing right next to you. Faith Chapel. Sunday night. Seven o'clock. Right?"

Eileen nodded eagerly.

"You make sure He's got His best stuff ready," Tom continued, "because Tom Canboro is coming to church and he's going to need a whole lot of convincing."

Suddenly Eileen's eyes narrowed. There had to be a catch. "And what if I do?" she asked. "Then what?"

Tom laughed. He knew his sister only too well. "Just promise me this," he concluded. "If I go there and sit like a good boy and listen without saying a word for the whole hour and I still don't believe . . . well, then, you've got to promise to get off my back. And stay off it."

"You've got a deal," agreed Eileen.

"I better go see about Suzie and Jason," Tom said after a minute. On his way out of the room, he turned for one more parting shot. "I'll tell you one thing that's true, Sis," he said to Eileen. "I'm beginning to feel like I'm about the only one in this whole world who's got his feet planted on firm ground. And I intend to keep it that way."

While Tom and his sister replayed their age-old argument, Suzie sat at her brother's bedside, holding his hand. He was calmer now that the drugs had taken effect, but there was still no mistaking the strange glint in his eye and the intense edge to his voice as he spoke in a low whisper.

"I'm sorry, Jason," Suzie was saying. "I did the best I could, but the doctors are very concerned. And considering what you tried to do, I can't say that I blame them. All any of us want is whatever's best for you, whatever it's going to take to make you better."

The look Jason gave his sister needed no words of explanation. *Why*, he was saying with his eyes, *can't you under-stand?*

"If you really want me to get better," Jason replied with quiet urgency, "then listen to what I'm saying. They took control of me back at the house. Don't you see? I didn't want to kill Eileen. That's the last thing I wanted. And I didn't want to jump out that window. It was them. They had control of my mind and my body. And now that their plan didn't work, they're going to come looking for me. Do you hear what I'm saying?" His voice was beginning to rise again. "They're going to come looking for me," he repeated.

Suzie sighed, unsure that she had the strength to argue with her brother anymore. "The doctors are worried about you, Jason. They're afraid you might—"

He cut her off with a savage jerk of his head. His neck muscles were bulging, and Suzie could see the veins in his temple throbbing.

"You're not listening to what I'm saying," Jason hissed. "Don't you see? If I really wanted to die, all I'd have to do is sit around here, waiting for them to find me."

Tom entered the room at that moment. Wordlessly he put his arm around his wife's shoulders, gesturing for her to follow him outside. When she stood up, he laid a comforting hand on Jason's leg.

"It's going to be all right, buddy," he said before turning and leaving with Suzie.

In the hallway outside, Eileen was waiting, and the three of them huddled for a family session to try to handle the crisis that had emerged in the midst of their once happy lives.

"He needs your help," Tom was saying to his wife. "It's obvious to everyone but you, Suzie. He's trapped in a world he can't escape from."

For reasons Suzie herself didn't understand, Tom's words roused her anger again. She felt as if she were fighting off attacks from every direction. "What makes you so sure that a bloodstream full of drugs is going to help him?" she demanded. "He's my brother, Tom, and he had a bad experience tonight. It could happen to any of us. What he needs is family, not Thorazine. Please. Let's take him home with us and just see—"

"We can't just take him home," Tom interrupted. "He's been put on suicide watch. He's got to stay here."

The words cut Suzie deeply. There seemed to be no way to counter the grim reality of a loved one who might take his own life. Tom reached and put his arm around her again. "Look, Honey," he said, "like it or not, Jason is going to have to spend at least one night in this hospital. Try not to worry. They're going to take good care of him. I'm sure of it."

A nurse rounded the corner carrying a tray with a hypodermic syringe and several vials of drugs. When Eileen saw what was about to happen, she stepped in front of the door to block the way.

"Could you please just hold on a few minutes with that?" she asked.

"But, ma'am," protested the nurse. "We need to begin the pro—"

Something in the nurse's tone of bland professionalism snapped the last cord of restraint in Suzie. "Look," she said, trying desperately to hold on to her own sanity, "I don't care about your procedures. I want to spend a few more minutes with my brother before you do whatever it is you think needs doing."

The nurse, confused and a little frightened by Suzie's ominous tone of voice, turned to Tom. He nodded reassuringly, and she scuttled back to the nurses' station where she picked up the phone to page the attending doctor.

On the other side of the door, Jason could hear the vague murmurings of his sister and the others. For a brief moment he felt reassured, knowing that he hadn't been left alone in this terrible place . . . at least not yet. But, even as the thought comforted him, he was shaken by the realization that in this very room he could sense another presence. Far from being left alone, there was someone close by, keeping watch over him.

Lifting his head off the pillow again, he was horrified to see that his worst fears had taken the shape of a man—a man with a shaved head, a goatee, and an earring, dressed entirely in black. It was Zack Probert, and as Jason's eyes widened in terror, a bleak smile grew across the mysterious stranger's thin lips.

"Wha—what do you want?" stammered Jason, hardly able to hear his own voice above the pounding of his heart.

Probert's smile never wavered. "Oh, come now, Jason," he said smoothly, his tongue flicking like a snake's. "You certainly know the answer to that question. I'm here for one reason: that the whole world would believe what you believed tonight. That's not too much to ask, is it?"

Frantically Jason readied himself to scream for help. *Now they will believe me,* he thought. *Now they will see for themselves the evil that was loosed on the world.*

But beyond the thick door to his room, no one would have had time to investigate the imaginary enemies Jason saw lurking in the shadowy corners. They were too busy struggling to comprehend their own set of incredible circumstances, the evidence of which the doctor was holding in his hands.

"Look at this," the doctor was saying, holding up a pair of CAT scan results for Tom, Suzie, and Eileen to study. "I've been in this business for a long time, and I can tell you honestly, I've never seen anything like this in my entire career." He held up one of the multicolored scans, showing a cross section of a human brain. A smattering of bright green was concentrated in a few key areas of the picture.

"Now," he said, "this is a scan of a normal human brain. The green areas show neural activity, in other words, functioning brain cells. As you can see, the part of the human mind that is actually working at any given time is rarely more than ten to twelve percent. As a neurologist, I can tell you that I have never seen that number go higher than one or, at the most, two points. Now this," he continued, holding up the results of a second scan, "is a CAT we took of Jason when he was first admitted."

The difference was immediately evident and remarkably striking, considering what the doctor had just told them. The photo was rich with large patches of bright green, clearly the dominant color and clearly evidence that had dumbfounded this medical expert.

"The activity in Jason's cortex is well over seventy-five percent," he said, trying hard to suppress his excitement. "If I wasn't seeing it with my own eyes, I never would have believed it. This man is showing active brain cells in parts of his mind that . . . well, let's just say this is a completely unprecedented development. Jason, quite simply, is a medical marvel."

At that very moment, all the brainpower of that medical marvel was directed toward one overriding goal—to survive the hideous threat to his life that glowered at him from the corner of the room. Jason could feel the malevolent power radiating from Zack Probert as if it were invisible rays bombarding his consciousness with deadly accuracy. He was having trouble thinking straight, and he could feel his breath constricting in his lungs.

"So you see," Zack was saying, as though explaining a simple lesson to a child, "it wasn't that our message was mistaken. No. It is the truth, completely and absolutely. Our only mistake was to introduce it to humanity too early. Let's face it, Jason. The world simply isn't ready for what we have to offer. At least, that is, it's not ready yet."

Zack's eyes closed slowly, and he bent his head in concentration, directing his deadly energy toward Jason, whose neck suddenly stiffened as the back of his skull slammed against the pillow and was held there. His breathing became even more labored and shallow, and as he gasped for air, the blood began to drain from his face. The bedside monitor to which he was hooked up began beeping loudly. A moment later, the doctor, with Suzie and Tom close behind, rushed into the room. They were followed, a heart-beat later, by Eileen.

The presence of the committed Christian in the room broke Zack Probert's concentration. Glaring at her, he stepped back into the shadows of a bed curtain partition and watched balefully as the others gathered around Jason's bedside. Eileen seemed to be the only one who noticed the clammy chill in the air, and shivering, she pulled her sweater more tightly around her shoulders.

"What are you going to do for protection when she is gone?" The words that Zack spoke seemed as if they had entered into the deepest chambers of Jason's mind. In fact, none of the others seemed to acknowledge his presence, and Suzie's frantic brother realized that, to everyone else, Zack was as invisible as the air they breathed.

"He's here!" Jason shouted, drawing breath back into his lungs. "Can't you hear him? Can't you see him? He's the one! The one they sent to deal with me!"

Mystified, the others looked around the room, scanning the beds, the steel tables and chairs, and an incongruous picture of a cartoon cat hanging from the wall. Tom considered that perhaps it was this drawing that Jason was insisting had spoken to him, and he cast a sympathetic eye in his brother-in-law's direction.

But Jason could not take his eyes from the corner where Zack Probert continued to fix him with a gaze like two burning embers. "Please," he cried, his voice cracking with agony, "please just leave me alone." He began to weep, a piteous sight, begging and pleading with his invisible tormentor. "I won't tell," he whimpered. "I promise I won't tell! Just don't kill me. I'll do anything"—sobbing racked his prone body—"just . . . don't . . . kill . . . me."

Suzie turned to Tom, a helpless look on her face. Whatever her arguments for Jason's sanity might have been a few minutes ago, it was clear to both of them that she was rapidly losing credibility. She sighed, defeated and demoralized. "Would you guys leave us alone for a moment?" she asked Tom and Eileen. "I want to try to make Jason understand why I have to leave him here tonight."

Throwing his jacket over the back of a chair, Tom gestured to his sister, and both left the room, taking their places just outside the door in the now deserted corridor. An empty wheelchair stood nearby, and with a motion that was half serious and half in jest he offered the seat to Eileen. When she declined with a smile, he shrugged and settled into the chair. No question about it: tonight's chaotic events made him feel more than a little as if he needed to be wheeled home and put into bed. It seemed to Tom that he could sleep for two weeks straight if he had half the chance.

He looked up at Eileen, leaning against the wall of the corridor. For all their disagreements, he felt a sudden flood of affection for her. At least she was someone he knew he could depend on, no matter what.

"Hey, Sis," he said, the weariness evident in his subdued tone. "I'm sorry about losing my cool back there."

Eileen waved his apology away. "It's okay, Little Brother," she said. "It's been a hard night for all of us."

"You've got that right." Tom nodded, then shook his head. "Poor Jason. It hurts my heart to see him like this. I only hope they can find some way to help him this time, once and for all."

"Me too," Eileen concurred. "It's awful to see a person suffering so much. He seems terrified of his own shadow."

Tom pursed his lips into a thin, grim line. "I know Suzie means well, bless her heart," he continued. "But to tell you the truth, I think she's only going to make it worse if she starts talking to him about that Ouija board of his. I mean, once he gets going on all that paranormal mumbo jumbo . . ."

His voice trailed off as he saw an ashen look draw over Eileen's features. She pulled her sweater closer around her again although, as far as Tom could tell, the hospital corridor was stuffy and overheated.

"Don't tell me," he said, rolling his eyes. "God's got something against Ouija boards. Right?" But he was in no mood to pick up the argument where they had left off. Rising from the chair, he crossed to his sister and gave her a warm and spontaneous hug. "Never mind," he said gently. "Maybe I'll find out for myself when I go to church this Sunday."

A glance at his wristwatch confirmed the late hour. "Well," he said, releasing his sister from his embrace, "at least the window Jason jumped through was on the first story of our house. Can't do much damage from that height.

That other poor guy, the one who seems to have had the same idea as Jason, lived clear up on the fourteenth floor. I guess I better get down to the morgue and identify the body." He could see the worried look that crossed Eileen's face at the mention of a dead body, and he turned up his sister's chin and looked her in the eye. "Are you going to be all right?"

"I'll be fine," Eileen said. "You go on ahead." She watched as Tom disappeared down the long corridor, leaving her alone to wonder what forces and entities had been loosed in this place and why she could almost feel their cold breath on the back of her neck. They seemed to be surrounding her, invisible sentinels, waiting for their chance to strike.

Chapter 6

FOR SUZIE CANBORO, confused and conflicted about what was best for her disturbed brother, the night of terror and uncertainty seemed endless. She had been so sure, such a short time ago, that if he could only return home with her to the safety and security of familiar surroundings, he would certainly return to his right mind and become, once again, the brother she had known and loved since they were children, playing in the front lawn sprinklers together.

But then came Jason's strange and inexplicable behavior, the shouting and screaming, the sobs and choked pleas, the invisible tormentors and the paranoid response to each and every person in hospital scrubs. It was painfully clear that Jason was in no condition to go anywhere, and having to admit that reality made Suzie feel like crying in helplessness and frustration.

All that was left for her to do was to try to placate him, humor his weird requests until he was calm enough that she could leave him for the rest of the night. Jason's current demand was almost more than she could handle, however.

As she carefully lined the inside of his baseball cap with aluminum foil, she wondered if Tom hadn't been right all along. Maybe the best place for her brother was somewhere he could be properly looked after, treated by professionals and monitored on a twenty-four-hour-a-day basis.

"Is this what you want?" she asked, holding up the altered cap and trying to hide the concern in her voice. "Are you sure this is going to help?"

"Of course it's going to help," Jason snapped back at her. "Just hurry up and put it on my head. You never know when they might start transmitting. I've got to be prepared."

Suzie tried to ignore her brother's impatient tone and carefully placed the cap on his head, pushing it down until the foil formed a tight seal.

"Ah," said Jason, clearly relieved. "Now that's better." He looked up at her, gesturing for Suzie to draw close so that he could whisper in her ear. "They're still out there, you know," he told her, his eyes darting frantically around the room. "I'm not making this up, Suzie. You've got to believe me. These guys are for real."

"I know they are, Jason." A voice came from the doorway, and Suzie and her brother swiveled around to see Eileen standing silhouetted in the light from the corridor.

"There's more going on here than you can understand," she said to Suzie in a low, urgent tone. "Jason isn't crazy, Suzie. I know that's hard to believe right now, but he's tapped into something that's very real . . . and very dangerous. I think we should get him out of here. The sooner, the better."

Suzie stood up, her heart pounding. She didn't know

why and was sure it was against her better judgment, but at that moment, she knew Eileen was speaking the truth. It was now or never. Wordlessly she began to unstrap her brother's arms and legs, while Eileen stood watch at the door.

"Hurry," her sister-in-law urged. "We don't have much time."

Three floors below the ward where Eileen and Suzie were carrying out their desperate plan, Tom ambled down another hallway, following the signs that pointed to the morgue. The turmoil that had been boiling in his mind all night seemed to have subsided, at least for the moment. Suzie had agreed that the hospital was the best place for Jason; he had made his peace with his sister, Eileen, even though it would cost him a Sunday evening in a church pew when he would have preferred to watch whatever game was featured on ESPN; and most important, he had a romantic anniversary at Rat Lake to look forward to with his wife. Maybe things would work out for the best, after all.

Pushing open the heavy steel-reinforced doors of the hospital morgue, Tom immediately felt the chill that was meant to preserve the corpses for as long as possible in a constant temperature. He was about to call out for an attendant when he noticed the shadows of two men, side by side in the room just beyond where he stood. They were talking in low tones, and Tom's seasoned police instincts sent him a very clear signal: a little eavesdropping was in order.

Moving stealthily to within hearing range, Tom was careful to keep his presence hidden from his surveillance subjects. Although the men's faces were hidden in shadows, he could hear every word they said. As their conversation continued, whatever sense of well-being Tom clung to vanished like the morning mist.

"Some guy from over on Campbell Avenue," said the first man, and from his profile it was chillingly clear that he was one of the minions of Zack Probert who had gathered around the Babel tower not three hours before—the one called Morgan Scott.

"How?" was the one-word question from his companion, who stepped from the shadows momentarily to reveal himself as another of the mysterious coven of men in black cowls—Carl Sweig.

The one called Morgan shrugged. "Search me," he answered, and Tom wished he could do just that. As his eyes adjusted to the dim light, he could see posted on a light box mounted on the wall another of the CAT scans swarming with bright green patches of color. "I didn't think such a thing was even possible."

Who are these men? Tom asked himself. *And what are they doing down here?* He kept his eyes and ears peeled, watching and listening for clues that might answer his questions.

"So who was it?" Carl Sweig probed.

"Wait until you get a load of this," Morgan replied. "It was Suzie Canboro's brother. Small world, isn't it?"

At the sound of his wife's name, Tom felt a hot flush of anger rise up inside. If these guys thought they were going to get Suzie involved in whatever they were up to, they had another think coming.

"And you mean to tell me he picked up on the whole thing?" asked the one called Carl.

Morgan nodded. "That's what it looks like," he answered. "Apparently he jumped out the window just like our late psychic phenomena professor, Mr. Tucker, here." He gestured to a shrouded body laid out on an autopsy table. "Too bad for us it happened to be on the first floor."

"You mean, he's still alive?" interjected Carl with fear in his voice. "We can't let him—"

Morgan held up his hand for silence. "It's under control," he reassured his partner. "Probert's on his way up there right now to finish the job."

That was all Tom needed to hear. Stepping silently back from the room, he turned and slipped through the heavy doors, breaking out into a run as soon as his feet hit the yellow waxed linoleum of the hallway.

Three tense minutes later, he burst from the elevator before the door had fully opened and rushed toward Jason's room. Bursting through the door, he took in the empty room in the blink of an eye, and turning, he began to run again. He might still be able to stop them somehow. At that moment he heard a familiar voice coming from the open window of the room.

"Taxi!" shouted Suzie. In three giant steps Tom was at the window, pushing aside the billowing curtains just in time to see Suzie and Eileen climbing into the backseat of a taxi. Jason, holding his foil-lined hat firmly to his head, sat between them.

In the second it took for the taxi to pull out of the drive-way and accelerate down the empty street, Tom struggled with a mix of emotions. First, he felt vast relief that whoever was after Jason and Suzie hadn't caught up with them yet. At the same time, he had to suppress his anger at the fool-ish action his wife, sister, and brother-in-law had taken. Whatever the threat to their safety or their very lives might be, there was nothing Tom could do about it until he was able to catch up with them and make sure they were taken out of harm's way. He had to get to them . . . and get to them quick.

But before that could happen, he'd have to shake the two men whom he had overheard in the morgue. He heard them even now, emerging from the elevator and striding straight toward the open door of the room. In the next split second they appeared in the doorway, and it was immedi-ately clear that, however Tom might have felt about his missing family, these men were equally intent on getting to them—if for very different reasons.

"Where is he?" barked the one called Morgan. "What happened to the man in this room?"

"And who might you be?" was Tom's implacable response. Morgan reached into his jacket pocket and pro-duced a shiny badge in a leather case, flashing it in front of Tom's eyes too quickly for him to read what might be writ-ten there. "And what exactly do you want with Jason Quincy?" the unimpressed Tom continued.

"That's none of your concern, Officer," spat back Morgan. "Now, if you'll be kind enough to take us to him, we'd be very appreciative. We're busy men, and quite frankly we don't have time for your—"

"They're up in X ray," Tom interrupted, coming up with the plausible lie in a flash of inspiration. "I've been told they'll be back down in about fifteen minutes." He shrugged. "But I wouldn't count on getting much information out of him if I were you. Last time I saw him he was rambling on about space aliens and some other gobbledy-gook. They had to knock him out with a heavy dose of tranquilizers just to get him strapped to the bed."

Morgan nodded and turned to flash a quick look at his confederate. The news was obviously just what he wanted to hear. "Thank you for your help, Officer," he said. "Now, if you'll be so kind, we'd like to have a few more words with you while we're waiting. Do you have a problem with that?"

"Not if you're willing to tell me what this is all about," countered Tom.

Morgan shook his head and crossed his arms in front of him. "I don't believe we're under any obligation to answer anything, Officer. As federal agents, we clearly are the controlling authority in this situation. It's my firm understanding that you, as local law enforcement, are required to provide whatever assistance I and my associate might require."

As he spoke, Tom moved casually toward the open window as if he were seeking a breath of fresh air. A glance down at the street confirmed his hopes: the taxi was nowhere in sight.

"I'll repeat," he said, turning from the window. "What is this all about?"

Morgan swallowed hard. It was clear he was not used to being disobeyed by mere beat cops. "I must know immediately who else might have heard any of that nonsense Mr. Quincy was spouting," he ordered.

From the door behind him, the doctor appeared. He had overheard at least the last part of their confrontation.

"According to the ambulance driver," he said, trying to be helpful, "Jason was talking about—"

Tom held up his hand, silencing the naive physician. "Thank you, Doctor," he said loudly. "That will be all."

The doctor departed, but not before throwing Tom a reproachful look. As far as he was concerned, he'd only been trying to help. *That's what you get for being a nice guy*, he thought as he continued his rounds.

With the offended doctor out of the way, Tom turned his full attention back to the so-called federal agent and his partner. "Now tell me again," he said laconically, "why is it so important to find everyone who might have heard what Jason Quincy was saying?"

But Morgan was only half listening, having turned in the direction in which the doctor had retreated. "Did he say that the ambulance driver heard him?" he asked the one they called Carl. His associate nodded and, producing a walkie-talkie from his coat pocket, stepped into the hallway as the device in his hand crackled to life.

"What about at the house?" Morgan said, turning back to Tom with a snarl. "Did anyone hear what he was saying at the house? I need an answer, Officer. And I need it now."

"Not until you tell me what this is all about," Tom

declared stubbornly. "I mean, what possible difference could the ramblings of a disturbed man make to the federal government? He's a psychiatric patient, for Pete's sake."

From the corridor, Carl rushed back into the room, still holding the communication device. He gave Tom a quick but penetrating look before gesturing for Morgan to follow him back into the hallway. Once alone, the two conferred in whispers, glancing frequently at the door to make sure Tom stayed exactly where they could find him.

"I got the rundown on that cop in there," Carl reported in low tones.

"What about him?" asked Morgan. "He seems harmless enough. Just another stupid—"

"He's more than a cop!" interjected Carl.

"What are you talking about?" demanded Morgan.

Carl took a deep breath. "He's Quincy's brother-in-law. Suzie Canboro's husband." He nodded, acknowledging the shocked look on the confederate's face. "That's right, Morgan," he said. "That so-called stupid cop has heard everything."

Morgan didn't wait to hear any more, but charged back into the room where Tom was supposedly waiting patiently for their return. "Detective Canboro," he said, pulling out a gun from his shoulder holster, "my associate has just informed me that Jason Quincy is actually your—"

He stopped. The room was empty. Rushing to the window, he looked down on the street. It, too, was devoid of any human presence. Looking around frantically, he kicked open the bathroom door. It took him only a moment to see that the facilities were shared by the adjacent hospital room and that the door between the rooms was wide open.

While Morgan and Carl were rapidly putting together the circumstances of Tom's escape, the detective was racing across the parking lot, making a beeline for his car. But his progress was delayed by the sight of an ambulance parked in front of the emergency exit, its lights flashing madly and its siren blaring like a wounded banshee. What struck him as odd was that there were no paramedics rushing to the scene, no gurneys, and no ER crew to hustle the patient into the hospital. As he passed the unsettling scene, he glanced through the window and into the driver's side of the vehicle. A man lay with his head slumped back against the headrest, his eyes glazed and his mouth hanging open. The ambulance driver was a victim of having heard whatever Jason said and whatever his pursuers wanted to keep a secret.

Swallowing hard, Tom sprinted the last few yards to his car, leaped inside and, gunning the engine, roared off into the night with a squeal of tires. Almost before he was out of the parking lot, he had grabbed the police dispatch radio and was phoning in an emergency message.

"Dispatch," he said loudly into the mike as he sent the car skidding around the corner and out onto the main thoroughfare. "This is Detective Canboro. I'm just leaving St. Joe's. There's been a ten ninety-nine there. Ambulance attendant in the parking lot. Better get someone over there pronto."

Dropping the radio mike, he reached into his pocket

and pulled out a cell phone. The car was weaving across several lanes of traffic now, running red lights as Tom desperately steered toward home. "Come on! Come on!" he muttered at the phone in his hand as he rapidly punched a series of numbers. He waited a moment until the canned voice of a message machine came on the line.

"Thanks for calling Tom and Suzie," said the message, unspooling in Suzie's sunny voice. "We're not here right now, but if you'd like, please leave a message and we'll be sure to get right back to you."

"Suze!" Tom shouted frantically into the phone. "For the love of God, get out of the house. Jason was right! He's been right all along. You've got to listen to me. Get out now!"

He threw the phone down on the seat beside him and reached for the radio microphone. Clicking on the "send," he was about to put out an APB on the taxi when he felt a strange and deadly sensation under his right foot. The gas pedal slammed to the floor without any pressure from him and the car lurched forward, gathering speed at a terrifying rate. He lifted his foot entirely off the accelerator, but the car continued its headlong rush down the road: 70, 80, 90, 95, 100. Tom watched with horror as the speedometer pushed itself to the limit.

Then suddenly from around the corner, a blinding pair of lights lit the compartment of the car. Tom looked up to see an eighteen-wheeler, its horn blaring loudly, heading straight toward him. He tried to turn the wheel, but like the accelerator, it seemed locked in place by a force more powerful than mere human strength. The truck came closer, then closer still. The moment arrived when Tom realized that, even if he could manage to regain control of his car, it was already too late. A full head-on collision was inevitable. The grille of the truck was right in front of his window, grinning with chrome teeth like an infernal beast.

The sound of crashing glass and the sharp shriek of rending metal filled his ears as Tom felt himself tumbling downward into a bottomless black abyss.

Chapter 7

THE PIT INTO WHICH TOM HAD FALLEN was steep and slippery, echoing with strange noises and unfamiliar sensations. From far off and high above him he could see a pinpoint of light, and he struggled with all his strength to reach it, swimming through empty space, floating closer and closer until the dot began to grow. First it was the size of a baseball, then a melon, then the moon, and finally the exit to a tunnel large enough for him to crawl out of and into the blindingly bright glare of consciousness.

Tom lay prone on a hospital bed, the muscles of his body aching as if he had been stuck in one position too long. As his eyes opened, the ceiling lights cut into his corneas like razor-sharp knives, and he gasped in shock and pain. *Where am I? What happened to me?* He thought back frantically to the very last thing he could remember, but it was all an indistinct blur. Something about a dead man in an ambulance, a fast ride in a car, and the headlights of something huge and unstoppable bearing down on him. After that, black numbness until this very moment when light at last penetrated his lids and his eyes tried vainly to adjust to the blazing light.

Gradually he was able to focus enough to be aware of the hum of machinery around him. He opened one eye, then the other, and with a groan that sounded as if it came from an eighty-year-old man, he lifted his head off the pillow. He couldn't remember ever feeling quite so old and tired. He could hardly hold the weight of his brain on the thin stalk of his neck. His joints creaked as he tried to rise again, collapsing back onto the bed and panting heavily before giving it another try.

At the far end of his vision he could see his feet sticking out of the blankets, and he wondered how long it had been since he had trimmed his toenails. A *long time*, he thought, judging from the craggy growth that sprouted from his toes. He watched his hand rise as if it belonged to someone else and grab hold of the metal railing of what was obviously a hospital bed. Moving his legs to one side of the mattress, he gingerly swung his feet over onto the cold tile floor and tried to rest his weight on them. Before he was halfway up, he felt something tugging at his arms and legs and, for the first time, noticed a tangle of electrodes attached to his body. Pulling them off like leeches stuck to his skin, Tom stood and shambled toward an open door on the far side of the room.

The door led to a small bathroom with a mirror over the sink. Crossing to it, Tom stared at the reflection in the glass, and for a confused moment, he actually thought he was looking at a portrait of an old and distinguished gentleman—

perhaps a biblical patriarch or a Civil War general. Shoulder-length hair framed the face, which was covered with a thick, bushy beard that reached down to the man's chest.

A long moment passed as he tried to make sense of what he was looking at, until, with a sudden dizzying start, he realized it was his reflection. Shock was followed by a flood of new questions. *How long had I been lying there? What happened to Suzie, Jason, Eileen, and the rest of my family circle? Have I been in a coma? Have weeks, months, or even years passed me by while I lay there, growing hair and getting older like some kind of modern-day Rip Van Winkle?*

He staggered back from the picture of himself as an old man and, groping for the doorframe behind him, staggered back into the hospital room. "Hello?" he shouted, his voice sounding parched and dry, like the distant cry of a desert wanderer. "Is anybody here? I need help . . . please."

From a darkened corner he heard the rustling of bed-sheets that signaled someone stirring. "Shhh," a voice urgently implored. "Quiet. They'll hear you."

Tom moved toward the sound of the high-pitched, trembling voice, and as he did, a small bedside lamp was turned on. It revealed a thin man with large bulging eyes and a receding chin. The right empty sleeve of his nightshirt was pinned to his chest, indicating a missing arm. Tom silently thanked his lucky stars for the sight of another human being, but as he eagerly moved closer, the man shuddered and pushed back on his bed, as if trying to avoid any contact. Tom stopped. Obviously his fellow patient was disturbed and agitated, although about what, Tom could only guess.

"I'm Tom Canboro," he said as calmly as possible. "What's your name?"

"Evan," the skinny man whispered. "Evan Blair. But that's not important now. The main thing is that you've got to keep quiet. Whatever you do, don't let them hear you. You better get back to bed as fast as you can . . . before they find out that you're awake."

"Who?" asked the mystified Tom, the flood of questions rising again. "What's going on around here? Where are we? How long have I been here?"

"No more questions!" said Evan, trying to bury his head in the pillow. "Just do what I say. Or you'll be sorry."

"Why?" Tom couldn't help asking.

"Because," answered Evan, his body beginning to tremble as if a cold wind had blown through an open window, "if they find out you're awake, they'll try to put the glasses on you."

Tom wasn't sure he had heard the frightened little man correctly. "Glasses?" he repeated. "What glasses? What are you talking about?"

"The glasses!" Evan insisted impatiently. "The goggles! Don't you know what's been going on around here, mister? Where have you been, anyway?" He stopped suddenly with the look of a frightened rabbit. In the distance, the scraping sound of a large metal door being opened echoed through the room. "They're coming," he said, his voice cracking with fear and tension, then turned out the bedside lamp.

"Now listen very carefully," he continued, his words a disembodied presence in the darkness. "These people . . .

they're not like you and me. You can't trust them . . . you can't trust anyone in the world these days. Do you hear me? No one. Not your family . . . not your friends . . . not even the one you're closest to in your whole life. And the worst thing is, if they catch you and put the glasses on you . . . you'll never be the same. You'll be changed . . . into one of them. Or you'll be dead. That's the only choice you've got."

"Okay, look, Evan," said Tom, his mind still reeling from the events of the last ten minutes. "I don't know what they've got you in here for, but I have a feeling I must be in the wrong ward or something. I was in a car wreck . . . at least I think I was. I don't need glasses. My eyesight is twenty-twenty."

From down the hallway the clump of heavy boots drew nearer. "I don't have time to explain," insisted Evan. "Just get back into bed if you know what's good for you!"

Tom shook his head, adamant even in the darkness. "I'm not going anywhere until I find out what's going on around here," he countered, adding as much to himself as to his fellow patient, "I've got to find my wife. Maybe she'll be able to tell me what happened. I need to talk to some-one who's not—"

"Nuts?" Evan interjected. "Is that what you think? Listen, pal, I may be nuts, but I'm all you've got right now. Sure, I've been on a bender ever since the vanishings, but I still know what's going on. I was lying low until they caught up with me last night. And now"—his voice fluttered in fear—"the goggles are on their way."

"Vanishings?" Tom asked. Something about that word gave him an uncomfortable feeling. "What vanishings?"

Directly outside the door to their room came the unmistakable sounds of scuffling. Then, breaking into the darkness like shattering glass, came a man's defiant shout, loud and courageous. "Do what you want with me!" the voice cried. "But you know you can't win! I've read the book all the way through to the end. You'll never change what was intended to—"

The loud report of a gunshot put an end to the outburst, and Tom jumped, his heart in his throat. As the sound of a collapsing body resonated through the door, he hurried back to his bed, throwing on blankets and closing his eyes. Evan's warning had finally sunk in.

"You go right," Evan whispered loudly from across the room. "I'll go left . . . and good luck."

Through Tom's tightly shut lids, he could see light leak in from the door as it opened with the sound of jangling keys. Squinting just enough to see who had entered, he watched as two beefy men in black uniforms entered the room and, crossing to Evan's bed, lifted him out.

"Any word on how long we're going to wait for the other guy to wake up?" one of the team asked.

"No," the other answered. "If you ask me, they ought to just let us kill him and get it over—"

Before he could finish his sentence, the guard was knocked backward over a chair as Evan leaped out of their arms and, flailing wildly, bolted from the room and started running down the hallway. The guard on the floor jumped up, and the other took off after the escaped patient, followed quickly by his partner. Alone now, Tom looked up from his bed and saw that the keys had been left in the door lock. Getting to his feet as quickly as his weak muscles would allow him, he staggered toward the door, out into the hallway, and onto a waiting elevator.

While Tom made good his escape, Evan was running blindly down another hallway that ended in a cul-de-sac piled high with cardboard boxes full of medical supplies. In a panic he turned like a rat trapped in a maze to find another exit route, but it was too late. The two guards appeared around the corner, and while one tackled the thin one-armed man, knocking him into the boxes, the other approached slowly, holding up a strange and futuristic pair of goggles with a form-fitting headband and thick metallic frames. Evan struggled vainly as the spectacles were clamped onto his skull, but as soon as they were in place, his thrashing and moaning stopped. He lay motionless and silent on the floor, a small red light blinking from the center of the contraption on his head.

Although Evan might have been physically present on the hospital floor, surrounded by upended cardboard boxes, his mind was worlds away. When he opened his eyes, he found himself standing in a vast white expanse, with no walls, floors, or ceilings, no sense of up or down, right or left. But what caught his attention and brought an amazed gasp to his lips was a sight he never expected to see again: his missing right arm. There was no greater miracle for Evan Blair than to see himself whole again, lifting his restored limb high and flexing fingers he thought he had lost forever. Incredulous joy bubbled up inside him, and he wasn't sure whether he wanted to laugh or cry when suddenly, as if out of nowhere, a figure stepped in front of him. The familiar face of Franco Macalousso smiled at him benevolently.

"I know you," said Evan, pointing with a finger from his new right arm. "You're Macalousso! Franco Macalousso . . . they say you're the messiah."

"Hello, Evan," replied Macalousso with a voice that seemed to come from everywhere at once. Evan was not exactly sure the charismatic world figure had even moved his lips, or if he had just imagined that Macalousso had addressed him by his first name.

Macalousso smiled as if reading every thought that raced through Evan's brain. His immaculately tailored suit had a sheen like the scales of a reptile, and the touch of gray at his temples made him seem like the wisest and most compassionate sage Evan had ever encountered. Turning from Macalousso's mesmerizing stare, he looked again at his miraculously restored arm.

"My arm," he said, his voice choking with emotion. "It's impossible. How . . . how did you do this, Mr. Macalousso?"

The suave figure before him just shook his head. "That's the wonder of it all, Evan," Macalousso said. "I didn't do anything. You did it. You did it all. Don't you see, that's what I've come to show you . . . to show the world. It's what most of humanity witnessed for themselves on the Day of Wonders. And now . . . well, let's just say that there are only a few of you left who still need to be enlightened. For one reason or another you still haven't come over to our side. But those reasons don't matter anymore, now that you've seen for yourself what awaits you. When you finally make the right decision—and, believe me, you will—you will join with the rest of mankind in tapping into the wondrous powers that lie sleeping within us all . . . only waiting to be awakened."

"B—but," Evan stuttered, "I saw what happened to everyone who put on the glasses that day. They all seemed so—" He hesitated.

"Committed?" Macalousso interjected, supplying the word Evan was groping for. "Committed to bringing us all together as one united and harmonious mind? Think about it, Evan. Think about a world where anything you believe, you can achieve. It's that simple. All you have to do is believe . . . to give yourself over to that belief. Take my mark, Evan, and anything you can possibly imagine, everything you've ever wanted, will be yours."

Evan swallowed hard, his eyes glazing over as he let his imagination soar with the possibilities Macalousso dangled before him. The right choice seemed so simple, so obvious. He wondered why he had fought it so hard all this time.

As Evan faced his moment of truth and deception, Tom had arrived at the basement laundry room of the hospital. Stepping into the warm, damp air spewed by an industrial bank of revolving dryers, Tom was stopped in his tracks by a large poster tacked to the wall. A picture of a familiar structure dominated a landscape swarming with people from

every nation and tribe, gathering from every corner of the
earth to marvel at the Tower of Babel. A quotation unfurl-
ing from a banner overhead spelled out the message loudly
and clearly:

"Now nothing will be impossible."
Genesis 11:6

Puzzled but, more than anything else, vaguely disqui-
eted by the poster and its message, Tom moved toward a row
of lockers at the far end of the laundry room. There, high in
a corner, a television had been mounted, and whoever had
been watching it had left it on. Searching through the lockers one by one, Tom kept an eye on the TV screen, where
Franco Macalousso, sitting behind an enormous mahogany
desk, faced the camera and spoke in an even and measured
tone, his photogenic face inspiring confidence and security.

"Our destination," Macalousso was saying, "yours . . .
mine . . . all of us together, is a world where anything we can
imagine will be ours. Imagine, your greatest desires granted
in the blink of an eye . . . your yearning and hungers satisfied forever. If you haven't yet pledged your allegiance, body
and soul, to the great work we have undertaken, then the
time to make the right choice, my friends, is now. Like a
wonderful new dawn, the Age of Man is dawning. If you're
ready to be a part of the future, don't hesitate. Come into the
light. And if you're already a part of our great crusade, then
get ready to shine, my brothers and sisters. Because the first
day of the rest of your lives begins now!"

As Tom watched, confused and disturbed by what he was hearing, the face of Franco Macalousso on the TV screen suddenly dissolved into a blizzard of static. A moment later, another face appeared, that of a man Tom had never seen before. There was a calm certainty to his appearance, an urgency to his voice that was balanced by the clarity and conviction that could be heard backing up every word. Superimposed on the screen beneath the face were the words

JACK VAN IMPE
Recorded October 1999

"Don't be fooled, my friends," Jack Van Impe warned. "For when the Prince of Darkness makes his appearance here on earth, he will do so with incredible signs and wonders. In fact, this man will lie to the world with such conviction that the vast majority of those who have been left behind—" The message was interrupted as the screen went blank and the sound of static hummed over the speaker.

What did he mean when he spoke of incredible signs and wonders? Who was the man who would lie to the world? And what about those who had been "left behind"? Tom wondered if he would ever find the answers to the questions swirling through his brain. But there was no time to stop and try to sort it all out. If everything Evan had said was true, those men would be after him next. And they'd more than likely be bringing those goggles along with them.

Chapter 8

A BATTERED BLUE VAN SAT PARKED behind a screen of scrubs and small trees just off a two-lane road deep in a dense patch of forest. Outside, birds chirped and squirrels gathered their winter's supply of nuts and berries, and nature continued its endless cycles of rebirth and renewal. The late afternoon sun cast deep shadows through the branches of the trees, creating a peaceful and undisturbed natural setting in sharp contrast to the tense activity and banks of electronic broadcast equipment inside the van.

A satellite dish had been propped on the dash near the driver's seat of the van, and in the back three people intently watched the image of a man on a small TV screen. One of them was Suzie Canboro, and the transformation she had undergone since that fateful night when she disappeared into the darkness with her brother in the back of a taxi was both remarkable and profound. A serious purpose and powerful commitment had brought a new determination to her features, hardening the line of her jaw and giving her eyes a steely glint. But there was also a distinct trace of sorrow, as if she had borne a great loss and had not yet had the time to grieve for the ache in her heart. Somehow Suzie seemed older, wiser, and sadder.

Squatting next to her on the floor of the van as they huddled around the screen was her TV partner, Helen Hannah. While the change in the broadcaster's face was less dramatic than that of Suzie, it was clear that Helen had undergone some harrowing ordeal in the past days and weeks. Her glamorous TV aura seemed more down-to-earth now; the glitz and glitter that had been part of her star status had disappeared behind a businesslike expression. Helen was here for one reason and one reason only: to fulfill a vital mission.

The third member of the portable pirate broadcast station was a beefy black man with a good-natured expression whose deft handling of the complex machinery all around them singled him out as an experienced television technician. Jake Goss was his name, and by the familiarity with which the trio worked together, it was evident they had been a team for some time.

Suzie, Helen, and Jake were intently monitoring the same Jack Van Impe broadcast that had hijacked the Macalousso message Tom had seen in the hospital laundry room. The volume had been turned down so that they could hear one another's urgent instructions as they shot the televised beam from the VCR through the satellite dish and out into a waiting and watching world.

"We're up again," Suzie was saying as she watched dials jump with electric charges. "It looks like we've managed to take over the feed from the Fonthill transmitter." She turned to Goss. "What's our range, Jake?"

The technician glanced down at a laptop computer near the console. "I'd say about twelve hundred miles," he answered. Making a few swift calculations on the keyboard, he reported, "That gives us about twenty million people, give or take a few hundred thousand."

Helen looked over to her partner, expecting to hear a word of encouragement. Instead, she found Suzie absently turning the gold wedding band on her finger. "Not bad," Suzie said. "Not bad." Her thoughts, Helen realized, were far away, back to another time and place.

"Yeah," replied Goss, shaking his head and pursing his lips. "Only problem is, we're too late for about nineteen million of them."

Helen cleared her throat. It was time to put a stop to all this negative spin. "I think what you mean to say, Jake," she gently scolded, "is that it's a good thing we're not too late for a million other people. Let's not forget," she added, trying to bring them both into her positive frame of mind, "not everyone's on Macalousso's side. Not yet, anyway."

Jake nodded and, with a tilt of his head, acknowledged Helen's point. "You're right, Helen," he admitted. "It's just, you know, so frustrating. We're out here with this Mickey Mouse setup, trying to reach a few million folks, when what we really need to be doing is getting the word out to the whole world."

"That's not going to happen," said Suzie grimly. "Not without direct access to the transmission satellite."

"Listen, you guys," Helen said, not yet ready to give up on changing their point of view. "All we can do is the best we can. And for now, that means getting the word to as many people as possible . . . no matter how big or small that number may be."

On a panel overhead, a buzzer sounded loudly. "That's it," said Suzie. "They've started the trace." She turned to Jake. "How many relays along the line this time?" she asked.

The buzzer sounded again, and all three turned to look at it with alarm. "Thirteen," Jake reported. "But they're getting good at this. It's a little too close for comfort, if you know what I mean."

The buzzer sounded a third time. "It looks like it's twelve now," Suzie reported in a low voice even as the buzzer let off another ominous blast.

"Eleven," Helen said. "If I had to guess, I'd say they're close to figuring out our routine. We better get ready to roll the minute they start jamming us." With practiced efficiency the trio turned to their assigned tasks, putting aside, at least for the moment, the doubts and fears that trailed them like exhaust from the tailpipe of the battered old van.

Back at the hospital, Evan Blair would never again have reason to doubt or fear. A new certainty had grown in him, as surely as a new arm had sprouted in the empty sleeve of his shirt. Anything he wanted he could have. Any desire would be instantly gratified. If Franco Macalousso could bring back his missing arm, the savior of mankind would be able to accomplish anything. Evan Blair had found his messiah, his guide, and his spiritual teacher. He freely gave his heart and mind to Macalousso and his wonderful dream of world unity.

And the very least he could do was to prove his loyalty any way that he could. Removing the virtual reality goggles from his head, he sat up and, blinking back the bright light in the hallway, pointed toward the room that he and Tom had shared. The number 666 was evident, burned into the back of his right hand. "He's awake," Evan said.

It was all the guards needed to hear. While one hurried back in the direction they had come, the other flipped open his cell phone and hit auto dial for headquarters. It was only after they had left in pursuit of their prey that Evan noticed, for the first time, a mark like a brand imprinted across the top of his hand. Curious, he held it up to the light, wondering when and where the number 666 had been etched into his flesh.

In a distant room in the giant penthouse suite where Zack Probert oversaw the operations of the Macalousso empire, a phone could be heard ringing insistently. But Probert was in no mood for idle conversation. Picking up a newspaper that lay on the huge table where the Tower of Babel model still sat, he shoved the headline under the nose of his minion, Carl Sweig. "Haters on the Loose!" the paper screamed above two old publicity shots of Suzie Canboro and Helen Hannah.

"You idiots!" Probert ranted. "Why can't you find these two criminals and put a stop to their treasonous transmissions?" A fine sheen of sweat was glistening on his head. It was obvious that Probert was being put under scrutiny, and Carl didn't have to guess that Franco Macalousso was the one applying the pressure.

"They move so fast," Sweig replied helplessly. "By the time we can trace the point of their transmissions, they're gone . . . long gone."

"Then you'll just have to get there faster, won't you?" Probert snarled.

At that moment, Morgan Scott, another member of Probert's inner circle, burst into the room. "Yes?" said Zack Probert impatiently. "What is it, Agent Scott?"

Morgan stopped in his tracks and took a step backward. He recognized only too well that his boss was not in a mood to be trifled with. "Sir," he said, briskly snapping to attention. "I wanted to call to your attention that police officer who was trying to interfere with our experiments before the vanishings."

"You mean that moron in the coma?" Probert demanded. "What about him?"

"Well, sir," continued Morgan, swallowing hard, "it seems he's . . . awake."

"I'm confident your next words will be that he has come over to our side, Agent Scott," the bald man in black sneered.

"Not . . . exactly, sir," the agent replied fearfully.

"What?" shouted Probert incredulously. "Do you mean to tell me, the idiot chose to die instead?"

"Not exactly, sir," Morgan continued after exchanging a nervous look with his partner, Carl. "You see, they never quite got the goggles on him. In fact, I just got a report that they found his bed empty a few minutes ago."

Both agents could almost see the slow fuse of Probert's rage getting shorter by the second. "Well, then," their superior said in a voice as low as a snake's hissing, "I suppose you two better stop wasting my time and go find him." He looked down at the newspaper, realizing with a pleasant sensation how this latest development might just play into the solution to his more pressing problems.

"Perhaps," he said, as much to himself as to his hapless underlings, "he'll be looking for the same thing we are."

While Probert plotted his course of action through all the devious corridors of his twisted mind, a familiar face peered from the shadows of a doorway in the lower levels of the hospital. With a razor he had found in the laundry room locker, Tom had shaved off his long beard and hacked away at his shoulder-length hair until he was a reasonable facsimile of the man he was before these incredible events had begun to change his whole reality. He had exchanged his hospital gown for street clothes also borrowed from a locker and, with his new identity intact, made his way carefully toward the front doors of the hospital.

He was within twenty feet of his goal when the two guards, one still carrying the sinister goggles, appeared suddenly around a corner. Ducking from sight, Tom held his breath as they stood discussing their next move in front of the sliding glass doors that led outside to freedom. With only a matter of moments before he was discovered, Tom pushed open a door behind him and entered a doctors' lounge where an untended television had been left on. The image on the screen was, once again, Jack Van Impe, speaking with all the sincerity and authority that truth imparts.

"In the not too distant future," the renowned pastor was saying, "an incredible time will come upon the whole earth, a time such as mankind has never seen before and will never see again. It will be a dark period marked by the deepest delusion, trickery, and deception. And it will be the most dangerous time for God's creation since the beginning of the world."

As intrigued as Tom was with the compelling message of the pirate broadcast, his attention was drawn to a sudden motion in a shadowy corner of the room. Taking a step closer, he was amazed to see a middle-aged man sitting on the floor in a yoga position. Paying no attention to either Tom or the television, the mysterious individual was giving his full concentration to a book that was lying in front of him. Unsure what to make of this bizarre character, Tom began stepping backward as quietly and carefully as possible, hoping to get out of the room without being noticed.

But before he could retrace his steps, he was witness to an incredible occurrence. The book, which seemed to be the center of the man's entire focus, rose very slowly from the floor. Tom watched as the intense concentration on the man's face brought up large beads of sweat. The effort of levitating even this slim volume was taking up the last ounce of psychic energy at the individual's command. After lifting no more than six inches from the floor, the book collapsed, and the sound of its falling seemed to snap the man out of his trance. While the man blinked back the effects of his efforts, Tom slipped out the door, leaving it open behind him.

"Hello?" the man said groggily, staring up at the open door. "Anyone there?" With no answer, the would-be levitation master shook his head and went back to his brain-straining exercises.

The image of Jack Van Impe on the television screen in the doctors' lounge was mirrored on the small screen glowing in the dim light of the pirate broadcast van, which now sat in deep twilight alongside the road of its woodland hideout. As Suzie, Helen, and Jake watched, the pastor's intent features vanished from the screen and were replaced, seconds later, by a message from station WNN reading: "Technical Difficulties: Please Stand By."

Suzie was turning her wedding ring again as the broadcast came to an abrupt end. She quickly looked over to Helen. "How long?" she asked tersely.

"Four minutes and fifty-three seconds," Helen replied with a glance at her watch.

Suzie nodded with satisfaction. "I think that's our best yet," she said.

"Let's just hope somebody heard it," interjected Jake as he turned in time to see Helen give him a reproachful look.

"I'm sure someone heard it, Jake," she said. "Let's just pray that whoever did was listening to what was being said."

For Tom, the difference between hearing and listening would have been more than he was able to absorb at the moment. The only thought that he could identify jolting his brain was the near animal urge to escape the hospital with all its nightmarish scenarios that only confused and frightened him. He was sure if he could just free himself from its walls, he could find someone, somewhere, who would explain all the strange and spooky things that were happening. Reality was just beyond the doors of this place, and he had to reach the other side or die trying.

Racing frantically down a hallway, Tom turned a corner only to see the two guards not more than twenty feet from him. They turned in time to catch a glimpse as he fled in the opposite direction. Immediately the chase was on, and Tom's terror was heightened as he heard the sound of gunshots and felt bullets whistling by inches from his ear. Passing a dumbwaiter built into the wall of the corridor, Tom made a split-second decision. With gunfire erupting all around him, he took a dive into the narrow passageway, tumbling down a long metal tunnel and falling headfirst onto a delivery ramp. Getting unsteadily to his feet, he spotted an exit sign on the other end of the ramp and crossed to it as fast as his unsteady legs would carry him.

But before he could reach his destination and the safety he prayed was just beyond, a figure stepped out to block his way. There was something familiar about the tall man dressed in black, something about his bald head and silver earring that prodded Tom's memory. Skidding to a halt, he scurried back in the direction he had come, heading toward an open fire door that, as if by an invisible hand, slammed shut in his face. One by one, his escape routes were being cut off. Despite his desperate hammering, he could not dislodge the door, and as he turned his head to look over his shoulder, the shadowy figure still watched him. Tom wasn't sure if he actually heard a peal of evil laughter or just imagined it, but he didn't take the time to find out. Rushing across the hall to yet another door, he saw it slam shut seconds before he reached it. He knew better than to try, but hoped against hope that the handle would somehow turn when he grabbed it.

Like every other means of eluding the terrifying figure in black, this door was shut tight. This time, there was no question that the laughter he heard was real, a harsh, echoing sound that grew louder with every passing moment until it drowned out even the sound of slamming doors on every side of him in the hallway. The figure in black—the figure of Zack Probert—began moving toward him, the laughter echoing inside his head.

At the last possible moment, at the last possible door, Tom found a way to slip from Probert's infernal grasp. At the end of the hallway, a door stayed open as he rushed toward it, slamming as soon as he had pushed his way through.

Behind him, the laughter abruptly stopped. Probert rushed up to the exit through which his intended victim had escaped. Grabbing the handle, he forced open the door and entered a cool, dimly lit room with a broken window at one end. There, through the shattered pane, he stared down into the hospital parking lot where Tom Canboro was rushing toward the street and into the bustling city beyond.

Muttering a dark curse, Probert left the room and slammed the door so hard that a sign reading PSYCHIATRIC EVALUATIONS fell to the floor. Beneath, just barely visible, were the painted-over outlines of another name, a name that had once set this room apart as a place of sanctuary: PRAYER CHAPEL.

Chapter 9

I T WAS A CITY HE'D KNOWN for most of his adult life, a place where he'd gone to college, graduated from the police academy, met his wife, and moved into their first apartment. Here, on these very streets, he had gone to work each day, patrolled them as a rookie cop, and learned every shortcut, back alley, and boulevard from downtown to the city limits. It was his city, and although Tom and Suzie had moved to the suburbs shortly after his promotion and the raise that went with it, bought their own place, and become friends and neighbors of a whole new group of people, a part of him would always call this city home.

That was why, as Tom put one block after another between himself and the hospital, ducking down side streets and cutting across vacant lots to get as far away from that strange and hellish place as possible, he began to wonder whether he had somehow stumbled into the wrong city. Perhaps he had been moved after the accident. Perhaps these streets, for all their familiar names and landmarks, were actually part of some other urban sprawl—a place much darker and dirtier than he remembered the city he called home.

Graffiti covered every wall and bus bench, litter blew down empty streets on a foul-smelling wind, and piles of garbage blocked the sidewalks and spilled into the streets. Storefronts were closed and shuttered, or else burned out and abandoned. Lurid neon signs flashed in neighborhoods where before ordinary citizens had strolled the avenues on a warm summer's evening. Now these same blocks were choked with bars and peep show emporiums, video game parlors and adult movie theaters. Drunks lay in doorways, and prostitutes accosted anyone who happened by. Gang members flashed their strange and menacing signs, and the gutted remains of cars sat at the curbs, stripped of their tires, their windows shattered. Ragged children wandered from condemned buildings in a daze, and old men sat on doorsteps, staring into empty space. If this was the city Tom knew and loved, it had undergone a change so terrible and cruel that the farther he traveled into its heart the more lost and alone he felt.

He rounded a corner where there had once been a prosperous shopping district, which was now nothing more than the blackened shells of buildings and their riot-torn foundations. There, high above the street, a huge billboard was lit with garish lights. At the sight of it, Tom stopped dead in his tracks, his mouth dropping wide open.

Depicting huge blown-up likenesses of his wife, Suzie, and Helen Hannah, the billboard proclaimed the message:

WANTED FOR CRIMES AGAINST HUMANITY.
DO YOUR PART.
REPORT ALL HATERS.

Tom's befuddled mind, still foggy from his long coma, reeled at the sight of the gargantuan wanted poster. *What have Suzie and Helen done? Why are they called haters? And as a sworn officer of the law, am I obliged to "do my part" if and when I ever see them again?* The questions stabbed at his brain like sharp forks in the hands of angry children and he started to move away, still intent on getting as far from the hospital as he could. He was stopped by the sound of squealing tires and the loud metallic rending of a car crash behind him, and he spun around to see a dreadful scene unfold.

At the corner not far from where he stood, a police car had smashed into the rusted heap of an old jalopy that looked as if it had already had several accidents under its fan belt. As a second squad car came to a rubber-burning stop near the crash site, the door of the battered car opened, and a man, his face covered in blood from its shattering impact with the windshield, staggered out onto the street, dazed and half blind from the red gore that ran into his eyes. Stumbling and falling, the man rose again to his feet, but by then it was too late. A fleet-footed cop had tackled him, and both men skidded on the filthy pavement. The bloody man, obviously desperate to escape, punched and kicked at the officer, scrambling to his feet and resuming his headlong rush down the street.

As Tom watched helplessly, a second cop jumped from his police vehicle and, shouting, "O.N.E. Freeze!" took aim and got off a clean shot that shattered the fleeing man's knee. At that point Tom noticed for the first time the unusual black-and-gray-trimmed uniforms the policemen wore, not at all like the regulation wear he was familiar with, especially since the sleeve of each jacket bore an insignia that read O.N.E.

Tom hardly had time to catch his breath, much less puzzle out the meaning of the strange initials. The wounded man, still unwilling to surrender, dragged himself along the littered streets until the cops rushed up and, kicking and punching his battered and bleeding body, finally subdued him. It was then that the more vicious O.N.E. police officer reached around to a small satchel he carried on his back, produced a menacing-looking helmet with goggle attachments, and shoved it on the dazed and bruised man's head.

"No more running and hiding for you, pal," the cop sneered. "Your fence-sitting days are over. It's time to put up or shut up." He laughed. "You've got a choice to make."

The moment the goggles were in place, the bleeding man ceased struggling and lay as still as death. The police officers stepped back, satisfied with a job well done. Tom was about to move to avoid the risk of being noticed when he felt a tap on his shoulder. Turning around to see who had sneaked up on him, he was hit without warning with a jarring blow to the jaw and fell heavily to the street.

Lying on his back, Tom looked up to see a hefty

man standing over him, holding an umbrella as if he were a batter looking for a grand slam. Although the light was dim, Tom could clearly make out the bold black marks on his assailant's hand—three numbers, all the same: 666.

Smiling as disarmingly as possible, Tom nodded at his attacker and slowly and carefully held out his own hand as if to demonstrate that, whatever club the numbers 666 made you a member of, he'd already joined. In the split second it took for the man with the umbrella to cast a glance at Tom's hand, he moved with lightning speed and academy-trained reflexes to sweep his legs under the man's feet and sent him crashing to the ground.

Bellowing with rage, the man staggered upright, ready to deliver a deathblow with his umbrella. But Tom was nowhere to be seen, and in the sudden eerie quiet of the dark street, the only sound was a low groan from the bleeding man with the goggles on his head.

Even while the scene on the street was being played out with violent and life-threatening intent, the bleeding man from the battered car had entered into another reality entirely—a world of white, with no up or down, top or bottom, walls, floors, or ceiling. It was a world inhabited by only two people: the man with the goggles and the familiar figure of Franco Macalousso.

In the pure white space between them another creature stirred—a deadly cobra, hooded, coiled, and ready to strike. It was then that the voice of Franco Macalousso seemed to fill the vast white void.

"It's just a matter of what you believe, Ronny," he said, addressing the man whose bleeding forehead seemed to have been miraculously restored. "And how strongly you believe it. Try it for yourself. You'll see."

Hesitantly, the man named Ronny closed his eyes. When he opened them again, the snake had disappeared.

"See?" said Macalousso with an oily smile. "It's all within you. The power is yours if you only ask to receive it." He took a step forward. "All you have to do is take my mark upon your body. And the gift you will receive in return will stagger your imagination. Anything you wish for will be yours instantly."

He put his arm around Ronny, the gesture of a father or a friend. "You see, Ronny," he continued, "these silly goggles are just a way of letting you see what is possible to all those who willingly follow me. They give you a glimpse of what a truly united world will be if you only believe along with the millions of others who are already walking my path. You've had a taste of it already. I know you have. You've seen people being physically healed. But even more important, you've seen others who have begun to realize the true potential buried in the human mind. Don't you see, Ronny? Once the last of the unbelievers, the haters, have been removed, then we will be free to create a paradise on earth. And to live forever . . . as gods."

For a moment, Ronny seemed to seriously consider Macalousso's words and the offer that he held out like the most succulent and tempting fruit. But then, with a sudden violent motion, he shrugged off the arm around his shoulder and took a step back, facing his enemy with a light of righteous fury blazing in his eyes.

"You're very smooth, Macalousso," Ronny said contemptuously. "Very smooth indeed. With your powers, your charisma, I can see why so many people have fallen for your pack of lies. But let's face it. We both know what's really going on here. A holocaust by any other name is still mass murder. Who's kidding whom? Your white room and magic snakes are very impressive. But I know what you're really after . . . what you've been after from the very beginning. You're interested in only one thing . . . to exterminate the people of God. It's as plain as the ponytail in your hair, Macalousso. Why don't you just go ahead and get it over with? I'm not afraid of you. You can do what you will with the body. It's nothing but flesh anyway. But my soul, the real treasure God has given me and the only thing that really interests you, that you can't touch. Because I choose not to give it to you, not for any of the false promises you make."

As Ronny bravely spoke out the truth, Macalousso's normally implacable expression grew dark and mottled with rage. The thin facade of love and compassion gave way to stark hatred, and he vanished from Ronny's sight. In his place, the deadly cobra returned, and with a hiss, it sprang forward, launching itself at Ronny's face.

Back in the real world, the O.N.E. police and a few bedraggled passersby watched Ronny's prone body, lying in a spreading pool of blood from his wounded leg. Without warning, his body stiffened and his hands clutched at his throat. Then, like air leaking from a punctured tire, the life seemed to seep out of his body. His hands fell away, revealing twin puncture marks aimed directly at his jugular vein.

While Ronny endured the final agony that was the price he had to pay for standing firm against the temptations of Franco Macalousso, Tom had fled far from the scene of the horrifying confrontation and soon found himself wandering aimlessly along streets that looked like the aftermath of an inner-city riot or a terrorist bombing. Everywhere he saw destruction and devastation, and his mind churned as he tried in vain to comprehend what had happened to his world in the time that he had been unconscious after the accident.

In that despairing state of mind he stumbled onto a long, dark alley, strewn with garbage and small fires burning in oil barrels to shed light and warmth on the population of homeless citizens who called this filthy and rat-infested backstreet home. Pushing past the cardboard huts they had erected for shelter, Tom tried to avoid the upraised hands grasping at him as if to strip the very flesh from his bones. Faster and faster he hurried through the maze of hungry, dirty faces until finally he broke into a run, cold sweat pouring over his body. As he fled, he heard the voice of an old man behind him, calling out forlornly like the last witness of a terrible catastrophe.

"They're gone," the haunted voice cried. "All gone. Millions upon millions of them . . . vanished into thin air. I remember the day. I remember it well."

Not far from the alley a rapidly approaching Zack

Probert, with Morgan and Carl in tow, was making a thorough sweep of the neighborhood with one target in mind—Tom Canboro. Probert knew that once Tom was in his hands, he could lay a trap to capture the most notorious hater of them all—the pirate broadcaster, Suzie Canboro, and her team. Reaching the shadowy length of the alley, he paused and signaled his thugs to follow him into its depths.

Sprinting with all his strength, panting and pushing his weakened muscles to the limit, Tom reached the back of the alley only to find his escape route blocked by a solid brick wall. Behind him, he could hear the sounds of voices and echoing boot heels. Trying hard not to panic, he turned to see the silhouettes of Zack and the others against the bright lights of the street behind them. Surrounded by the hulks of sleeping figures huddled under newspaper and lice-ridden blankets, Tom grabbed a tattered piece of yellow cardboard with green stripes, the torn box from a toy company delivery. He lay down in the grimy alley and pulled it over him, doing his utmost to calm his ragged breathing.

At the other end of the alley, Probert and his vicious team worked their way methodically through the homeless camp, tearing up the fragile huts and ripping off the flimsy coverings with which the denizens of the alley kept themselves warm. One by one, they searched every cranny and corner until Probert came across a large piece of cardboard, green-striped on a yellow background. Pulling it away, he revealed a man beneath, wearing a baseball cap and slumped over as if unconscious. As Probert reached down to rip the hat off, the man suddenly stirred and raised his arms over his head in a feeble effort to defend himself.

From down the alley, Tom, lying under his own piece of similarly colored cardboard, watched with dismay as Probert grabbed the man by the wrist.

"O.N.E.," he barked. "Let's see your mark." Quickly inspecting the hand he held and not seeing the telltale 666, he turned to Morgan. "Who's got the goggles?" he demanded.

"They're back in the car," Morgan reported. "I'll send someone to get them right—"

"Never mind," Probert interrupted. "The world we're trying to build will be better off without this kind of human scum, anyway." Pulling out a revolver, Probert took point-blank aim at the man's face and pulled the trigger with no more concern than if he were brushing a fly from the spotless lapel of his custom-tailored suit.

The killing of the homeless man unleashed an orgy of violence among the three searchers. Gunfire echoed through the alleyway as homeless people, orphans, and others unlucky enough to be in the wrong place at the wrong time were ruthlessly gunned down. The choking smell of gunpowder and the groans of the fatally wounded reached Tom as he trembled in his hiding place, his face pressed close to the stinking asphalt. His options were only too clear: to stay where he was and face summary execution at the tender mercies of the bald-headed killer and his squad, or to make a break for it. Knowing it was better to be killed trying to save his life than to lie there like a willing sacrifice, Tom threw off the cardboard and, without looking behind, squeezed down a narrow passage between two buildings. Behind him he heard the screams and gunshots echoing in the humid night air.

Chapter 10

To Tom's fevered and increasingly disoriented brain, it seemed as if he had been on the run forever. Streets and boulevards began to blur and blend together, a mad kaleidoscope of blighted buildings and wasted faces, staring at him with a mix of curiosity and hostility. He no longer had any idea of where he was going, how he would get there, or what he would do when he arrived. The only purpose in his life for the moment was to keep moving, to walk and walk and never look back for fear of what might be gaining on him.

The night seemed to stretch on forever into areas of the city he couldn't remember ever being in, even in his earliest days as a cop on the beat in the roughest parts of town. Just when it seemed that his legs might give out underneath him for good, he spotted a phone booth across a street where people seemed to be milling about aimlessly. Moving across to the corner where the booth stood, he slipped inside and picked up the receiver. Immediately an automated voice came on the line.

"Identify yourself," it commanded with none of the pre-recorded pleasantness he was accustomed to. Suddenly from a slot beneath the keypad, a tray slid out into view. Imprinted on it was the shape of a human hand and the instructions: *Place Right Hand Here*. Desperate to place a call to his home where he could only hope Suzie might still be waiting for him, he was about to obey the command when his eye caught sight of a poster pasted to the glass wall of the booth on which the message was emblazoned:

WORLD UNITY IS A SHARED RESPONSIBILITY.
WHEN YOU HEAR THE ALARM, DO YOUR PART.

Looking back down at the hand tray, then out at the people beyond the door of the booth, Tom thought better of giving himself blindly to this process of identification. While much about this frightening new world was strange and alien to him, he was beginning to catch on to certain survival techniques: foremost among them—keep a low profile. Returning the receiver to its hook, he slipped back out on the street and continued his relentless wandering.

Half an hour later, Tom stumbled into a shabby convenience store along a block that looked as if it had been firebombed. Trying to appear casual and conveying the impression that he was completely at ease in this nightmarish new reality, Tom knew that the confusion and apprehension he felt like the chill of a high fever could only be partially hidden. He tried to smile as the clerk looked up from behind the counter.

"Glory to man," the attendant said, his eyes already narrowing suspiciously.

"Yeah," Tom muttered. "Whatever."

"I said," the clerk repeated in a low and threatening tone, "'glory to man.'"

"Right," Tom said, realizing he had almost tipped his hand. "Of course. Glory to man. Listen, uh, friend . . . I need to use your phone. It's . . . very important. You know . . . official business."

The clerk looked at him blankly as if he were waiting for an explanation of Tom's unorthodox behavior. The unnerving expression on the clerk's face sent Tom's heart into his throat. The constant fear with which he had lived since awakening from his coma was beginning to take its toll. He had an overwhelming urge to laugh, cry, or scream.

"Look," he said, swallowing hard. "I need to make a call. I tried a pay phone, but it was . . . out of order. Please . . . it's vital that I get in touch . . ." His voice trailed off as he noticed the clerk staring at his hands. Thrusting them in his pockets to hide the absence of the three-number mark that seemed to be another one of those vital keys to survival, he looked back at the clerk with a weak smile. "Never mind," he said, backing out of the store. "It's . . . no big deal."

"Let me see your hand," the clerk said coldly.

"What?" Tom replied, playing dumb.

"Your hand," the clerk repeated. "Let me see it . . . right now."

Tom tensed, poised and ready to bolt when the clerk pulled a massive shotgun out from under the counter and pointed it straight at Tom's head.

"Hey!" he shouted, attracting the attention of a few forlorn shoppers in the rear of the store. "I've got one. Over here! I found a hater!"

"No," pleaded Tom, holding up his hands. "I'm not a hater. Glory . . . glory to man . . ." One of the customers, an overweight woman in a housecoat and rollers, came up behind him and, grabbing his elbow, jerked his right hand down to her eye level. Inspecting it for a brief moment, she shouted, "He hasn't got the mark! He hasn't got the mark!"

The clerk raised the gun and leveled it at a point directly between Tom's eyes. Barely realizing that his reflexes were working automatically, Tom sharply pulled his elbow back into the woman's soft gut. With a surprised groan, she fell backward. At the same moment, Tom grabbed the barrel of the gun and, yanking it from the clerk's hands, threw it across the store as he backed out into the street. Turning and running at full speed, he rounded the corner and a moment later had disappeared into the milling crowd.

It was early morning when Tom wandered aimlessly down a street that led to the outskirts of a park, as dismal and untended as the rest of the city. Dead grass was littered with garbage, and half-starved dogs walked the paths in packs looking for food. Several homeless people slept on benches and under the trees in encampments built of cardboard boxes and other debris. As Tom wandered through the devastation, he spotted a middle-aged man wearing a raincoat and talking into a cell phone as he sat on the edge of a bench also occupied by the hulk of a sleeping indigent. He studied the man for a long moment over the top of a newspaper he had picked up off the ground and pretended to be reading. An older couple walked slowly by, and a jogger with headphones dodged the ravenous dogs and piles of trash to stubbornly finish his run.

When Tom saw that they were at last alone, he put down the paper and approached the man who was getting up from the bench and heading toward the street beyond the park. Bumping into him as if by accident, Tom deftly lifted the cell phone from the man's pocket, then stopped and, with a vindictive look on his face, pointed to the figure of the jogger making his way farther into the park past a dried-up fountain. "Hey!" Tom shouted as loudly as he could. "That guy doesn't have the mark! I saw his hand! It's a hater! A hater!"

The startled man in the raincoat immediately did what Tom had hoped he would and set off after the jogger, shouting for him to stop and surrender. "Hey, you!" he screamed. "Hold it right there! Down with haters! Kill all haters!"

Hurrying in the opposite direction, Tom moved across the border of the park and found himself in a residential neighborhood that seemed in slightly better condition than the rest of the city. Ducking behind the garage of a large house on a corner, he punched a series of numbers into the cell phone and waited impatiently for the call to connect. An impatient sigh escaped his lips when he heard another recorded message, announcing, "I'm sorry. The number you have reached is no longer in service. Please check—"

Hitting the "disconnect" button, he spent a moment in desperate thought until another idea came to him. If he couldn't reach his home to find someone who could tell him what had happened to his wife, maybe his brother, Calvin, could answer the questions that had been plaguing him since he awoke what seemed like a hundred years ago . . . but was really a matter of only a few dramatic hours.

He punched in Calvin's number and waited for the connection, only to hear the same frustrating message. "I'm sorry," the recording blandly repeated. "The num—"

"Where is everybody?" Tom said out loud, then looked around, fearful that his voice would bring more of the unwanted attention he had been attracting.

Another notion occurred to him. Suzie and Calvin might be missing in action, but the police must still be on duty. He'd put in a call to the station house and try to connect with some of his coworkers. He dialed the number rapidly, and this time was rewarded by an actual human voice.

"City police," the female operator chimed. "How may I direct your call?"

Thank God, Tom thought, breathing a sigh of relief. He was finally on the right track. "Put me through to Detective Kenny Rice," he insisted. "It's urgent." If anyone could provide help and answers, it was his longtime partner, Kenny. They'd been through so much together, and even though

Kenny, like Eileen, kept bugging him about Jesus and salvation and all the rest, he was one of a handful of people Tom knew he could totally trust.

Which was why the next words from the operator came as such a shock. "I'm sorry, sir," she said. "There's no one here by that name."

Tom took a deep breath, swallowing his anger before he tried again. "That's impossible," he replied. "Check again. Maybe he's been transferred or something. Please, it's very important."

He could hear the operator sigh impatiently. "I've been here nineteen years, sir," she said with more than a little attitude in her voice. "There has never been anyone named Kenny Rice at this precinct."

Tom savagely hit the "end" button and hurled the phone into the street where it smashed against the pavement into a thousand shards. Once again Tom felt despair in his chest like a tightening vise. Where would he go now? What would he do? He was running out of options.

At that moment a strange realization dawned on Tom's exhausted and stressed mind. Standing in the shadows, trying to bring together his scattered thoughts into a coherent strategy, he realized that the tree-lined avenue he had wandered onto looked vaguely familiar. Moving cautiously from behind the garage, he stepped onto the sidewalk. With each step he took, the impression of recognition grew. He walked toward the nearest corner where a burned-out streetlight hung, and before he reached the end of the block, he knew exactly and precisely where he was. In all his blind

meandering, he had stumbled into the suburban neighborhood where he and Suzie had once lived.

Excited and hopeful now, he traversed the streets that
lay between him and his old home, anxious to see the
people and places that had once formed the core of his
world. Rounding the corner of the street where they lived,
Tom broke into a run until he reached, at last, the front
lawn of the house. There, all his hope and happiness
drained away like blood from a severed artery. Instead of the
cheerful lights and bustle of activity that usually greeted
him, the house stood dark and empty. On the lawn a sign
on a stake had been driven into the overgrown grass: FOR
SALE BY OWNER.

Shaking his head with sorrow and incomprehension,
Tom approached the front door of the house. It was locked
tight, and nothing stirred inside when he rang the doorbell.
Leaving the porch, he rounded the side of the house, and
looking around carefully to assure himself he was alone, he
balled up his fist and broke through the window of the
kitchen door. Reaching in to undo the lock, Tom didn't
notice his bleeding hand until he had stepped into the
room where he and Suzie, Calvin, Eileen, and Jason had
sat and talked that sunny morning. How long ago had it
been? A day? A week? A year? He had no way of knowing.

Pulling a jagged piece of broken glass from between the
knuckles of his hand, he reached into the clothes hamper
and found a T-shirt to wrap around his wound. For the next
half hour he carefully cased each room of the house, looking for a sign, a clue, any fleeting indication of what had

happened to his loved ones and why. Wherever they were, he decided, they had left very quickly. Dirty dishes were still piled in the sink, and a pile of laundry waited to be washed.

Discouraged and defeated, he sat down in the master bedroom where he and Suzie had spent so many comfortable and intimate evenings. Spotting the television remote control on the bedside table where it had always been placed before they went to sleep, he picked it up and clicked on the power. Feeling totally cast adrift, Tom had an urgent desire to hear a human voice . . . any human voice.

The screen came to life on a scene of a vast crowd gathering in a huge square. Images of happy and excited faces flashed by in sequence, and the enthusiastic voice of a newscaster narrated the unfolding events.

"This is your WNN reporter Wayne Goodwin reporting direct from the scene of tonight's worldwide telecast by Franco Macalousso." From behind him, the crowd could be heard roaring at the very mention of their messiah's name. "People from all over the country and, I may say, the entire world have been gathering here all week in anticipation of Franco Macalousso's historic address to Planet Earth. The anticipation has reached a fever pitch, and there is an aura of celebration surrounding tonight's speech, which is expected to be the culmination of Macalousso's worldwide campaign for a new and compassionate international order.

"We expect to hear a direct appeal from this great leader to all those who remain uncommitted, and it is certain that the enlightenment he has given to all of us will be made available to them as well. As for those who are already a part of this epic revolution in human consciousness, we will undoubtedly see the powers we have just begun to taste reach their full potential in each and every one of us who bear the mark of Macalousso and his crusade. We will blossom into beings with abilities and powers far beyond our capacity to imagine."

As excited as the reporter was becoming at the very words he was speaking, his tone suddenly changed as he brought a new and darker message. "But," he continued, "even at the dawn of this glorious new age, one can only wonder how the powers of negativity will react to the program that Macalousso has laid out. With the advent of the true messiah only scant hours away, fears that the haters are plotting to wreak havoc and destruction are gripping this crowd, just as they grip faithful followers around the world. Of course, top O.N.E. officials have been working around the clock to ensure that none of the poison and treason that the haters spout will interrupt Franco Macalousso at the moment he makes the most important announcement in human history."

Watching the broadcast, Tom was once again overcome with a feeling of dread. For all the talk of world peace, compassion, and universal harmony, the experiences of the past few hours, including the ruined city and broken and bleeding bodies of the homeless victims in a dark and dingy alley, made it all seem like a grotesque lie. Even as that potent emotion and the fear that came with it swept over him, the image of the reporter on the television screen began to fade and distort, finally dissolving into pure static before another face appeared, a face full of concern and conviction. By the time a name and date appeared to identify the face and the time of the recording—*JOHN HAGEE, JULY 1997*—Tom was completely engrossed in the man's words and the ring of truth they imparted.

"There will be many reasons not to follow Jesus Christ in the time of tribulation," Hagee was saying, staring straight into the camera as if he were speaking directly to Tom. "But always remember that the rewards of heaven far, far outweigh any pain you may have to endure here on earth. The choice that you will be faced with will be the one that decides your eternal destiny, once and forever."

In the reflection on the screen, Tom noticed a figure moving stealthily behind him, silhouetted by the moon that had risen to shine through the window. He shut off the television and, with the T-shirt still wrapped around his hand, retreated into the shadows in a corner of the room, crouching down to await whoever was stalking him.

Suddenly, with the sound of breaking glass, a man's booted foot smashed through the window. The next moment, a figure climbed into the bedroom carrying a gun. There was something hauntingly familiar about the man, and it took Tom only a moment to realize it was his next-door neighbor, Mike.

"Mike," he said, stepping forward eagerly. "It's me. Tom!"

"Tom?" was Mike's surprised reply. "I thought you were—"

"There's no time for that now," Tom cut him off. He had

already noticed with a sinking heart the fatal numbers 666 etched on the back of Mike's hand as he held out the gun. Whatever it meant to have those three numbers as an identifying mark, Tom had learned enough to know that it was the sign of an enemy he must fight with all the power and conviction at his command. "There's someone here in the house without the mark," he continued. "I just heard him walking down the hall."

Mike glanced down at Tom's hand, wrapped in the bloody cotton shirt, but before he could draw any conclusions, Tom had crossed to the bedroom door and was peering down the hallway. "I think he went this way," he told his neighbor, whispering urgently. "You've got the gun. You lead the way . . ."

Still uncertain of Tom's intent, Mike moved toward the door, and at the precise moment he passed Tom, he was hit from behind by a heavy tackle that send both men crashing to the floor. A desperate struggle ensued. Tom managed to knock the gun free from Mike's hand and send it skittering across the floor. The neighbor stretched out his arm, but the weapon lay just out of reach until, before Tom's astonished eyes, it began to move by the sheer power of Mike's concentration back into his grip. At the last moment before his finger reached the trigger, Tom landed a resounding blow to Mike's jaw, and as his opponent slumped, the gun stopped its mysterious movement.

Giving him another stunning shot to the face for good measure, Tom grabbed the weapon and stood up, straddling the dazed and bleeding Mike. Reaching over to a lamp on a hallway table, he disconnected an extension cord and used it to tie his neighbor securely to the banister railing. Still spitting blood, Mike slowly regained consciousness and looked up to see Tom staring down at him with a determined expression.

"Long time, no see," Tom said laconically. "Looks like you and I have a lot of catching up to do, neighbor."

Mike tried to clear his mouth of blood, spitting out a loose tooth as he started to speak. "You poor fool," he said with contempt. "You just don't get it, do you?" He laughed, a wet, wicked sound. "You act like you have some sort of choice. You have no choice, Tom. None at all. If we want to possess all the things that our great teacher has promised us, then we're going to require total unity from every living human being on the face of the earth. We are not going to let something as petty as family and friendship stand in the way of our great goal."

Tom was in no mood for lectures and resisted giving Mike another taste of his fists. "Where's Suzie?" he demanded. "Where's my wife?"

This time Mike didn't bother to answer; he only fixed Tom with an evil grin.

"Where is she, you idiot?" Tom shouted, raising his arm as if preparing to strike again. With no answer forthcoming, Tom deliberately cocked the hammer of the pistol and aimed it directly at Mike's head. "I'm going to ask you one more time," he said.

Mike stared defiantly back at him, seemingly unconcerned by the gun barrel pointed at him. Tom was considering calling his neighbor's bluff when, in the distance, he heard the sound of rapidly approaching sirens. In the next instant he deduced that Mike must have alerted the authorities before coming to the house. With the butt of the gun Tom knocked him cold and, leaving him limp and bloody at the top of the stairs, leaped over him, crossing the entryway and hurrying out into the only place left to hide—the darkness of night.

Before he vanished entirely, Tom stopped as if suddenly remembering something he could not afford to leave behind. Even as the sirens drew closer he rushed back through the front door and yanked open the hallway closet. Inside he rummaged through coats and winter wear until he found what he was after—the sport jacket he had worn the night before this nightmare had begun. Reaching into the pocket, he pulled out a small blue jewelry box and, opening it, allowed himself to gaze sadly at the diamond ring inside before he snapped it closed and hurried off again, scant seconds before the squealing tires of the police cars echoed through the empty neighborhood.

Chapter

11

WITH HIS SENSE OF DIRECTION and bearings finally restored, Tom headed unerringly toward the one place he could think of where he just might be able to rest and think long enough to restore his strength and plot his next move. Even as his shadows blended into the darkness of night, a low black car with O.N.E. emblazoned on the side screeched to a halt outside the Canboro home, and three familiar figures emerged, beginning with Zack Probert and followed by Morgan and Carl.

Hurrying to the wide-open front door, they made their way upstairs, stepping over the unconscious body of Mike as if barely noticing him. Splitting up his men to cover the house more effectively, Probert waited impatiently until Morgan and Carl returned empty-handed.

"Nothing, sir," Morgan reported, trying to keep the fear from his voice. "He may have been here, but he's gone now."

"Fools," Probert muttered, turning on his heel and heading back down the stairs as the other two tagged along looking sheepish. In the Canboro kitchen, Probert took in the broken glass on the back door and, after a quick search, discovered the now empty safe where Tom had kept his service revolver and holster. Spotting a tattered book with dog-eared pages beside the safe, he picked it up, brushed away the dust, and opened it. On the first page, he saw the name Eileen Canboro written below words that read, *This Holy Bible Belongs to.* He held it up like a trophy from a hunting trip and announced dryly to his men, "Good news. He's unarmed." The smile that spread across his face was a chilling thing to see.

Far from his familiar neighborhood, Tom pushed through the darkness, moving closer to his destination, even as the suburban streets began turning to country roads and the urban subdivisions gave way to open fields and forestland. The moon shed enough of a glow to light his way, but darkness descended everywhere else around him, which was why he passed by without noticing a battered blue van parked in a clearing behind a row of bushes and shrubs.

Inside the van, Helen Hannah was alone, huddled over the broadcast equipment and readying the transmitter for another pirate airing of Jack Van Impe and John Hagee. Pushing the "play" button on the VCR, she settled back to listen as Hagee's earnest face appeared on the screen.

"Heaven and all its glory is worth any sacrifice," the pastor and Bible scholar was saying. "Make sure you choose the gift of eternal life that comes only from a true belief in Jesus Christ. Don't delay another moment. Make your decision now, and give your life to Jesus Christ. Only He can save you in your hour of need."

Helen flipped a series of switches and two more faces appeared. The first was familiar—Jack Van Impe. The second, an attractive and sincere woman who shared the same calm certitude as the men, was Van Impe's wife, Rexella.

"Brother will turn against brother," Rexella was saying as Jack nodded in agreement. "And children shall turn against their parents. But the most frightening thing about this biblical prophecy is that they will do so thinking that they are making the right choice. Jack," she continued, turning to her husband, "just imagine a world so deceived and deluded that they will actually believe that peace and love and unity can come from killing and destroying those who stand in their way."

"Oh, and they certainly will, Rexella," agreed Jack Van Impe. "In fact, it was Jesus Himself who said in John 16:2 that 'the time cometh, that whosoever killeth you will think that he doeth God service.' There won't be a safe place on the entire planet for believers in the true God. This Antichrist will have complete control over the globe. It will be 'given unto him to make war with the saints, and to overcome them,' says Revelation 13:7. But to the rest of the world, he will seem to be the greatest spiritual leader that mankind has ever witnessed. Yet he's not who he seems to be. He's an impostor. A clever counterfeit of the true Messiah, our Lord, Jesus Christ."

At the mention of Jesus' name, Helen bowed her head in silent prayer. For so long she had resisted Him, and now, after all the shattering events that had taken place, she could only beseech Him to forgive her and accept her as she was, broken and needy.

"So, Jack," Rexella continued with remarkable insight, "if someone were watching a tape of this very program during the Great Tribulation, what would you want to say to them?"

Jack Van Impe turned and looked directly into the camera, his eyes sparkling with true compassion and wisdom. "Rexella," he began, "I'd tell them that it's not God's will that any should perish. I'd assure them that God loves the world and that He gave Himself for it. I'd urge them to believe that they who call upon the name of the Lord shall be saved—in our day as much as in their day."

His eyes seemed to ignite with conviction as the camera pulled in closer and filled the screen with Jack Van Impe's face. "If you are hearing my voice today," he said, "wherever you are, bow your head with me and let's just say this prayer together."

Along with Rexella, Jack closed his eyes. "Dear God," he prayed, "I am a sinner. I believe that You died for me. I ask You to come into my heart and into my life. Forgive my sins, I pray. In Jesus' name. Amen."

The camera returned to Rexella, who opened her eyes and smiled brightly. "Thank you, Jack," she told her husband. "And I would just like to add that it is in my heart today to encourage you all. No matter what your circumstances may be, know that God is greater than the problems you are facing. He loves you and has a plan for you."

As the Van Impes continued with their message of encouragement, broadcast across a gulf of time to a world in the grip of a terrible evil, shadowy figures toting impressive firepower began to merge into the clearing and surround the van. Moving closer, the lead O.N.E. officer whispered to his partner, "Well, well. Look what we have here. Helen Hannah and her renegade band of haters."

Pushing open the van door, he found his target on her knees, with her hands folded and her eyes tightly closed. Startled by the sudden sound of the sliding door, Helen gasped as the O.N.E. squad burst into the van and, grabbing her roughly, pulled her into the cold night air.

Not far from the unfolding circumstances that seemed to put an end, once and for all, to any message of hope for a world about to be plunged into darkness, Tom struggled through thick underbrush until he came upon a rise. Across an open field, he could see a small cluster of houses along a two-lane country road. He knew this place well—it was the little hamlet where his brother, Calvin, lived. It had not been the destination he'd had in mind when he rushed from his own home with the sound of sirens hot on his trail, but as he had made his way through the still forest night, his thoughts had turned, as if on their own accord, to his kid brother. Tom knew that, before he made another move, he had to see if his brother had survived the dreadful events that seemed to have engulfed the whole of existence.

Dirty, his clothes covered with clinging leaves and twigs, Tom entered the village and walked stealthily up the street. A man sitting before a picture window in his living room happened to look up just as Tom was nearing. Standing suddenly, he let the newspaper that was resting on his lap fall to the floor. There, once again, were the photos of Suzie and Helen that had been plastered on the billboard back in the city. The headline screamed, "Haters Threaten Messiah's Outreach to the Lost."

While the man watched Tom, he couldn't help rubbing his hands together in delicious anticipation. It was the moment he had been waiting for.

At the end of the block as Tom was approaching Calvin's house, he passed by a bright purple Volkswagen Beetle parked at the curb. *Well*, he thought with a wry smile, *some things will never change*. Arriving at the front gate of his brother's home, he opened it wide, walked up the path to the front door, and rang the doorbell. A moment later, Calvin flung open the door, a look of perfectly acted surprise on his face. He had just had time to hide the newspaper before the arrival of his long-lost sibling.

"Hello, Cal," said Tom warily, not knowing exactly what to expect.

Calvin seemed to be completely overjoyed to see his big brother and reached out to embrace him tightly, holding him with both hands, on one of which the inscription 666 had been deeply etched. "Tom," he said, appearing to choke back emotion. "Tom . . . I thought I'd never see you again!" He stepped back and gave his brother a long, lingering appraisal. "Let me get a good look at you," he said, even as his eyes dropped to Tom's hands.

Understanding exactly what his brother was looking for,

Tom held out his arms. "Is this what you're trying to see?" he asked, thrusting his hands under Calvin's nose. "No 666, Little Brother."

With a worried look, Calvin grabbed Tom by the shirt and pulled him through the front door and into the living room. "Quick!" he said. "Get yourself in here. And whatever you do, don't let anyone see you!"

Locking the door behind them, Calvin peered out the window before drawing the blind tightly closed.

"What's going on, Calvin?" Tom asked. "What happened to everything? What happened to me? And where is Suzie?" Once he started asking them, he could not stop the flow of urgent questions.

Calvin shook his head. "I haven't seen Suzie in a long, long time," he said. Then he added, "Believe me, I want to find her as badly as you do."

The news that Suzie was still out of his reach seemed to deflate Tom entirely. With a weary sigh, he sat down in a nearby chair. "What about Eileen?" he asked. "Where's Eileen?"

Calvin looked mystified. "Eileen?" he repeated. "Who's Eileen?"

For a moment Tom thought his kid brother was playing one of his famous pranks, a trick he was certainly in no mood for. But when he searched his face and saw only a blank look, the sickening conviction that his brother was serious caused the blood to drain from Tom's face. "Eileen!" he shouted. "Our sister!"

Calvin stepped back, nodding as if he had just verified

a sneaking suspicion. "The doctors warned us that this might happen," he said grimly. "Tom, you've had a very serious accident. You're not yourself." He leaned forward to emphasize his next words. "We don't have a sister, Tom."

"What are you talking about?" Tom's shout filled the house. "Of course we have a sister. We all grew up not far from here. We played together." His eyes filled with tears. "She was . . . wonderful."

Desperate to prove what he was saying, Tom looked around the room until his eyes fell on the mantel where there was a collection of family photographs in frames. He crossed over to them, and he was so anxious to see the evidence of his sister's existence that he barely noticed the boxes, each marked DANGER, EXPLOSIVES, piled on the living room floor.

A nagging doubt was beginning to grow in the back of Tom's mind as he made his way to the fireplace. Maybe he was crazy after all. Maybe this whole frightening new reality was nothing but a dream, or the delusion of a man with a severe trauma to the head. He was beginning to wonder whether he could even trust himself when he picked up a picture from the mantel and thrust it at Calvin.

"There," he said, pointing. "Who do you think this is?"

"Who?" asked Calvin, and he seemed genuinely mystified.

"Her!" shouted Tom, looking closely at the picture for the first time. A wave of shock came over him as he stared at the photo in his trembling hand—two young boys sitting side by side next to their doting mother and father. It was the perfect picture of domestic bliss except that the sister Tom so vividly remembered was nowhere to be seen.

"Never mind!" he said, his voice trembling as he picked up another picture. But the missing Eileen failed to materialize there, or in the next one, or in the one after that. Finally Tom picked up the last picture in the row—the same photo he had once had on the shelf in his kitchen, showing him and Calvin and Eileen down by the old oak tree in the forest. But in this version of reality, only Tom and Calvin stood under the broad canopy of leaves. Eileen was not there.

Devastated and now more sure than ever that his mind was failing him, Tom sank into a chair by the fireplace and put his head in his hands. He was so tired, so completely exhausted. All he wanted to do was to crawl away in a hole somewhere and sleep for a hundred years.

"What's happening to me, Calvin?" he asked his brother in low monotone. "What's going on? I can remember everything, every detail of Eileen's life. The way she looked. The way she laughed." He looked up at Calvin, his eyes wet with tears. "How could you forget? She was into all that religious stuff. We used to make fun of her. It's as clear to me," he swallowed hard, "as you standing there."

Calvin walked up and put his hand on Tom's shoulder. "Don't worry, Big Brother," he said. "You've got a few things to work out in your head after that accident of yours. It's really amazing you weren't killed by that truck. Just look at the bright side. At least we've still got each other. And you're still in one piece." He smiled. "And that means you've still got a choice to make."

Lifting his hand from his brother, Calvin extended it toward a table on the far side of the room where a wicked-looking automatic pistol had been laid.

As Tom turned to watch, the gun began to shiver and vibrate completely on its own before flying across the room and straight into Calvin's waiting hand.

"How . . . how did you do that?" Tom stammered, suddenly remembering the knife that had flown into the hand of the crazed college professor so long ago.

"What? That?" replied Calvin, grinning broadly. "Like the man says, Tom, 'You ain't seen nothin' yet.' This is just the beginning."

Tom could feel the nerves along his spine and into his skull beginning to snap. He couldn't take much more of this. He looked up at Calvin and spoke with slow deliberation. "Why don't you tell me exactly what is going on around here, Cal?" he said.

Calvin chuckled deep in his throat. "We're just getting a taste, that's all," he explained. "We're only just beginning to awaken the wonderful powers that lie sleeping within each and every one of us."

Tom shook his head in stark amazement. "They don't look too sleepy to me," he said with a whistle. "That gun moved over here faster than anything I've ever seen."

"Genesis 11:6, Tom," Calvin answered as if explaining a simple fact to a small child. "Once the people are united, nothing shall be impossible for them."

"'Once the people are united'?" Tom echoed. "What's that supposed to mean, Calvin?"

Training the gun on Tom, Calvin reached over to a nearby bookshelf and pulled down a pair of the same goggles that Tom had seen so often over the course of his harrowing day. "It's better to show you than to try to explain," said Calvin. "Once you put these on, all your questions will be answered. You will see the world and everything in it in an entirely new light."

"Those goggles sure seem to be important to people these days," Tom commented while the wheels of his mind turned over his options for the next few critical moments. He stared at the strange device as Calvin held it out to him, but made no attempt to take it from his brother's hand.

"Just trust me," Calvin invited him. "Go ahead. Put them on."

"And why would I want to do that?" Tom questioned.

Calvin's benevolent smile vanished. "Because if you don't," he snarled, "I'm going to blow your head right off your neck." He raised the gun a little higher, sighting it on a spot just between Tom's eyes.

"Don't you think that might be a bit extreme?" Tom asked, playing for time.

"Not in the world we live in today," Calvin replied. "There's a lot more at stake here than you could possibly imagine, Big Brother."

Tom stood up, his anger at the boiling point, and looked his brother straight in the eye. "Well then, Calvin," he said between gritted teeth, "maybe it's time someone shared it all with me."

Calvin pushed the goggles closer. "Put them on," he ordered.

"I don't want to put them on," Tom countered. "Put them on yourself."

"I have," said Calvin. "That's why I know they're the only way you will ever know the truth."

"And how about you, Calvin?" asked Tom. "Do you know the truth?"

"Of course I do." His answer was unwavering. "The truth has set me free."

"Then why don't you save us both some time and just clue me in on it?" Tom said.

Calvin smirked. "Because the only way you'll really believe is if you hear it directly from the messiah himself."

"Is that who's hiding in there?" Tom asked, pointing at the goggles.

"He's not hiding," Calvin snapped back. "He's there for anyone who wants him."

Tom pointed to the mark on Calvin's hand. "Is he the one who gave you that?" he asked.

"That," answered Calvin, "and a whole lot more."

Tom shook his head sadly. He could hardly believe that his brother had become so deluded. "What is it about the number 666, Cal?" he queried. "I mean, doesn't that send up all sorts of red flags for you? Don't you remember what Eileen said?"

"Don't start that again," groaned Calvin.

"And what about all that stuff?" Tom pressed, pointing to the boxes of explosives in the middle of the living room. "Are you going to tell me that's about unifying the world? You've got enough firepower there to blow the world to tiny little pieces."

Calvin sighed deeply. "Once again you fail to understand," he said. "There is a war on hatred going on all around us. And I've been given the means and the responsibility to level every church in this county."

Tom gave out a short, sharp laugh. "A war on hatred, Calvin?" he repeated. "Think about what you're saying. You're standing in front of me pointing a loaded gun at your own brother with a hand that's got 666 burned right into it. You can't even remember your own sister, and you're willing to kill the only person left alive in your family. What side of the war on hatred are you on, anyway?"

He gestured to the boxes that sat like coiled snakes ready to strike. "Are you some kind of a terrorist now or something?" he continued. "Is that it?" He shrugged. "I don't know, Calvin. I may be the one who had the head full of stitches, but it seems to me that it's the rest of the world that's going insane. And you're going right along with them."

"No," insisted Calvin. "You've got it all wrong. The world is just beginning to wake up. It is Lucifer, the only angel in heaven who ever truly had the interests of mankind at heart, who has come to show us the path to enlightenment."

"Lucifer," Tom repeated incredulously. "Lucifer?

Listen to yourself, you fool! Lucifer is the devil, don't you know that? He's Satan! Satan! The bad guy, Calvin!"

"That's a filthy lie!" shouted Calvin, waving the gun erratically. "There's nothing bad about him. Not even close. He is simply an angel who finally cracked the deep, dark secret of God. Don't you see? We can all achieve godhood. That's right, Tom, we can be gods ourselves! But of course, the so-called Almighty wouldn't stand for that. He could never let that happen. So when Lucifer let the cat out of the bag and told us the truth, he was thrown out of heaven and became branded as the enemy. Not because he did a single thing wrong. But because he dared to peek behind the curtain and see God for who He really is. A tyrant!"

"Come on, Calvin," Tom replied with a snort of derision. "What you're saying is just plain ridiculous. There's nothing in the Bible that backs up the fairy tale you just spouted."

"That's where you're wrong, Big Brother," was Calvin's confident answer. "That's exactly what it says in the Bible. If you ever bothered to read it, you'd know I was telling the truth."

Moving the gun closer to Tom's temple, he dangled the goggles in the other hand. "And if you knew the truth," he continued, "then you'd know that putting these on would be the best thing you could ever do for yourself . . . and for the world."

Fed up with his brother's high-and-mighty talk, Tom angrily knocked the goggles from his hand to the floor between them. "Right now," Tom countered, "I'd say the only big decision anyone has got to make will be you. What are you going to do next, Calvin?"

Deliberately turning his back on both his brother and the barrel of the gun pointed at him, Tom walked toward the door. As he crossed the room, he closed his eyes, hoping against hope that his brother would remember the bonds of blood between them—a connection that had once been the strongest thing in both lives.

He winced when he heard the click of the pistol's hammer falling on an empty chamber. So that was how it was. In the course of one day, he had lost his life, his wife, his sister, and now his brother. Calvin pulled the trigger five more times in rapid succession, and each time Tom's heart grew heavier until he felt like sinking to the floor and crying out for deliverance. He almost wished his brother's gun had been loaded. At least that way, he wouldn't have to face the loss and betrayal that tore at every fiber of his being.

Tom stopped walking and turned back to Calvin. "So that's the wonder of your enlightened new world, is it?" he asked bitterly. "You'd actually kill me, your own flesh and blood? You'd shoot me in the back, in cold blood. Is that the peace and harmony you're talking about, Cal?"

Reaching into his jacket pocket, he pulled out his service revolver and pointed it straight at his brother. A long moment of silence passed before Tom walked back to confront him. He gestured to the goggles on the floor. "Let me see those," he said.

For a brief moment, a kind of perverse joy filled Calvin's

face as he bent to retrieve the goggles. Then all went dark as Tom knocked him unconscious with the butt of the gun and left, walking out the door and into the night without looking back.

Chapter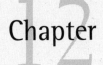

IN THAT DARKEST HOUR BEFORE THE DAWN, with the moon hanging high in the cloudless sky and the earth below still and sleeping, a lone figure approached the huge spreading oak in the middle of a forest meadow. The figure seemed to waver as he caught sight of the magnificent old tree, and a flood of memories shook his spirit to the core. It was the last place left to sustain him when everything else had failed and faded away. It might not have been home, but for this homeless man, it was as close as he was liable to come in a world that had turned hostile and murderous and ugly beyond all recognition.

Exhausted and frayed to the point of breaking, Tom's mind struggled with the emotions that overcame him at the sight of his favorite childhood haunt. Here he had spent endless carefree hours with Eileen and Calvin, swinging on these very same branches, sitting in the clover, and talking idly as the clouds passed by in fanciful shapes overhead. It seemed so long ago and far away, like the fond recollections of another man's life. If only he could go back to that time—to live again in those sunny and innocent days. That was his idea of heaven. He blinked back tears as he approached the tree.

At that moment he saw a familiar figure rise up from her place beneath the tree, her kind and gentle face glowing in the moonlight. With a cry that mixed the greatest sadness with the greatest exaltation, Tom rushed up to Eileen—the Eileen of those lost years, a fresh-faced and friendly thirteen-year-old girl in pigtails.

"Eileen!" Tom shouted. "It's you! I knew you'd find me!" Embracing his sister, he was amazed to see the arms of a young boy, in a flannel shirt that had always been his favorite, wrapped around her. Not only was Eileen restored to her youthful vigor, but he also had returned to the time of his childhood. It was like a dream come true. "Thank you," he sobbed as he buried his head in the soft down of her neck. "Thank you for finding me."

Eileen pulled back and looked at him with love in her eyes. "I didn't find you, Tom," she said, smiling radiantly. "You found me. And it's not me you should be thanking." She looked up to the sky, thick with stars. "It's God."

The young Tom followed her gaze through the thick branches and beyond into the twinkling vastness of heaven. "Thank You, Father," he repeated solemnly.

Those very words echoed in his brain as Tom awoke suddenly underneath the oak. Utterly drained from his horrific journeying, he had passed into a deep sleep as soon as he reached the sanctuary of the tree's limbs and trunk. There he had dreamed of his reunion with Eileen, a vision that seemed almost more real than the reality he awoke to.

Getting to his feet, Tom was struck with a sudden inspiration. Taking a book of matches from his pocket, he struck one, and in the brief flair of light he peered at an old carving, still set deep in the bark of the tree:

Eileen, Calvin, and Tom Canboro

July 1961

Overjoyed at the sight of their names, convinced at last that while the whole world might seem to be going crazy, at least he was still sane, Tom reached out and tenderly stroked the inscription. "Hey, Sis," he whispered softly as if he could still feel her presence from the dream, floating close to him on the soft, cool breeze. "You've got no idea how glad I am to see you." He vividly recalled the dream he had just had and the words he had spoken, thanking a God who suddenly seemed very real. *Too bad*, he thought bitterly, *too bad it was only a dream*.

Or was it? Tom's jumbled thoughts turned over and over as he grappled with feelings and ideas that seemed too large for him to hold on to. It was then, as the frustration and anguish welled up inside, that he lifted his voice to heaven and shouted at the top of his lungs, "Are You up there? Is anybody up there?"

"I am," came the response in a voice that Tom immediately recognized.

"Jason?" he asked tentatively as he peered up into the leafy canopy.

A rustle of branches and the sudden, surprising appearance of his brother-in-law, plopping down before him like an acorn dropped from its branch, made Tom want to shout for sheer joy.

"Jason!" he shouted again. He never thought he'd be so happy to see his crazy in-law in his life, but even wearing the baseball cap lined in foil that Suzie had fashioned for him, Jason was still a sight for sore eyes. "Man, am I glad to see you!" Tom exclaimed.

But Jason looked puzzled. "And who might you be?" he asked.

With a sinking sensation, Tom looked down at his brother-in-law's hands. His fear turned to excitement, however, when he saw that Jason was free of the dreaded symbol of surrender, 666. When he looked back, he saw a broad grin spreading over Jason's face. He was up to his old tricks, Tom realized. Stepping up to him, Tom delivered the biggest, hardest hug he had in him.

"When did you wake up?" Jason asked when Tom had finally let go of him. "We didn't think you'd ever get out of that coma."

"But," Tom answered in confusion, "you didn't know I was going to be here? I mean, weren't you looking for me at this spot?"

Jason scratched his head under its layer of foil. "Looking for you?" he repeated. "I wasn't looking for you. I thought you were looking for me." He pointed up to the tree. "I haven't been to this old place in years." They stared at each other for a long moment. Their meeting was too miraculous to be a mere coincidence. Something—or Someone—had guided them both to this rendezvous on this very night. "Well," Jason said at last. "I guess we've got Eileen to thank for that."

"Or maybe . . . God," Tom ventured.

Jason nodded, although the look on his face told Tom he wasn't quite sure of the truth behind that remark.

"You've got to tell me, Jason," Tom continued. "I've been going half crazy trying to find out what happened since I had my accident. The whole world seems turned upside down."

Jason's eyes got big. "It's just like Eileen used to talk about," he said in an awestruck tone. "She knew what was going to happen before it happened. It must have been all that Bible reading she did."

"You mean"—Tom was almost afraid to say the word—"the Rapture?"

Jason shrugged. "I don't know if it was the Rapture. All I can say for sure is that one day, she just disappeared . . . along with millions of other people around the world." He was getting excited now. "It was incredible, Tom! I was right there, standing beside her. One minute we were talking and the next"—he snapped his fingers—"she just vanished. Then the next thing any of us who got left behind knew, Franco Macalousso was on TV and radio and in the newspapers, saying that he was the one who had come to save the world. I believed him, Tom. We all believed him. Well, almost all of us. Then we started seeing what he did to people who refused to be part of his plan and wouldn't take the mark on their hands."

Tom nodded grimly. As fantastic as it sounded, it was all beginning to come together. "And Suzie?" he pressed Jason urgently. "What about her?" He grabbed his brother-in-law by the arm. "I've seen the billboards, Jason. I know she wasn't one of those who vanished. But what has she done to be branded a criminal? Where is she? How can I reach—"

He stopped, noticing the confused look on Jason's face. He'd been asking too many questions too quickly. "Is she okay?" he asked again, more slowly this time.

Jason nodded. "She's all right," he answered.

"Where is she then?" Tom continued, trying to contain his excitement.

Once again Jason looked blank. "I have no idea."

Tom mentally counted to ten. Getting useful information from his brother-in-law was like pulling teeth. "Then how do you know she's all right?" he asked with exaggerated calm.

"I happened to see another uplink this afternoon," Jason replied. Now it was time for Tom's face to take on a blank expression. Jason smiled. "I guess you've got a lot of catching up to do," he commented.

An hour later, Tom and Jason were walking along a forest path by the light of the moon, deep in discussion. Jason was right—Tom did have a lot of catching up to do, beginning with the incredible events that had occurred since the simultaneous disappearance of millions upon millions of the earth's population and the subsequent rise of Franco Macalousso and his soon-to-be-announced plans for perpetual world peace and universal government.

Grateful to have his questions finally answered, even though Jason's attention often wandered to odd insights and unrelated observations, Tom was anxious to find an explanation for one of the most disturbing and unnerving circumstances that he had encountered in his recent adventures.

"Jason," he asked, "why is it that no one with the mark on his hand seems to remember any of the people who vanished? It was so weird when I talked to Calvin about Eileen. It wasn't like he was pretending. I honestly think he'd forgotten that she ever existed."

His brother-in-law shook his head. "I wish I knew," he said. "It's all some kind of weird mind warp that happened to all of them. I'm sure it's got something to do with Franco Macalousso and his powers."

"And this Macalousso," Tom continued. "Does he actually claim to be Satan?"

"Lucifer," Jason corrected him.

"Same difference," Tom said. "But how come nobody seems to care?"

"I wouldn't say that," Jason cautioned. "It's not that they don't care. Ninety-five percent of all the people left on the planet believe with all their hearts that Macalousso is the savior of mankind. They're convinced he's a good guy."

"'A good guy'?" repeated a mystified Tom. "But how could that be?"

Jason stopped and turned to face Tom directly. Far overhead an owl hooted in a tree, and the night wind stirred the branches in the forest around them. "What would you call someone who claims to be able to reveal the secrets of the universe . . . secrets that God is supposed to have hidden from us all?"

Tom could see the point, but couldn't help wondering why Jason hadn't signed on to Macalousso's program. He would have seemed to be the perfect candidate. "What about you, Jase?" he asked. "I don't see the mark of Macalousso on your hand. That must mean you're not buying what he's selling." He smiled. "But, on the other hand, if you'll excuse the pun, you don't exactly seem to be rooting for God, either."

Jason was still staring at Tom with a look that was beginning to make him feel uncomfortable. "After tonight," he said, "it really isn't going to matter what I believe or whose side I'm on."

"Why?" Tom wanted to know. "What's so special about tonight?"

Jason started walking again. He was silent for a long moment as if trying to collect his scattered thoughts. "Do you remember," he said at last, "a while back, in your kitchen as a matter of fact, when I was telling you and Suzie and Eileen and Calvin about those monkeys that were on an island and washed the sand off their bananas?"

"Sure," Tom responded. "It seems like it happened last night."

"Well," continued Jason, and Tom couldn't help being impressed by how clearheaded and articulate his brother-in-law suddenly seemed, "that's exactly what Franco Macalousso is doing, Tom. I've figured this whole thing out, his big plan and everything. All he has to do is get enough people to believe what he's saying and—presto—just like those monkeys on that island, the rest of us will believe it too. We won't have individual thoughts anymore. It will all be one big group mind. We won't have to worry about making choices because there will be no choices left to make. And that's what tonight is all about."

"I . . . think I see what you're getting at," Tom said, struggling to wrap his brain around the incredible theory that Jason had just laid out. "But I still don't understand why everything depends on tonight."

"You're missing my point," insisted Jason with intensity. "The reality that we live in now is that this whole united consciousness method really works. And not just on monkeys." He stopped again and put his hand on Tom's arm. "What do you think happened to me when I jumped out that window on the night of your accident, Tom?" he said.

"I—I . . . really . . . don't know," Tom stammered.

"You probably thought I was insane," Jason continued. "That I was plain nuts. Delusional. Making it all up. Right? But I wasn't." He leaned forward as if to emphasize his next words. "Believe me, Tom, when I tell you that I had thoughts and commands planted in my brain. I was driven to jump out that window by a power greater than my own will."

Jason pointed to the hat with its foil lining on his head. "Why do you think I wear this?" he queried. "For my health? I'm telling you, I got an order to kill Eileen, for crying out loud. And the awful truth is, I would have done it. I simply had no choice."

Tom nodded, seeing the sincerity in his brother-in-law's face. "I believe you," he said. "I really do." He paused, the vivid memory of events earlier tonight returning to him. "I've seen what they did to Calvin. If that can happen to my own brother, it can happen to anyone."

"It's happened to virtually everyone else in the entire world," Jason commented somberly.

"But you still haven't told me what's going to happen tonight that will change everything," Tom insisted. "If all they have to do is send out a telepathic command, then why hasn't that last five percent of the world come over to Macalousso's side?"

"That's what I've been trying to tell you!" Jason said impatiently. "They have to get a majority of people thinking together . . . the same thoughts at the same time. That's been holding them back." He scoffed. "Oh, sure, they can spin pencils and move coins across a table, but do you think they're going to be satisfied with that? Of course not! They're after nothing less than the promise spelled out in the book of Genesis."

Tom nodded. "Let me guess," he said. "Genesis 11:6. Right?"

"That's the big payoff for Macalousso and his followers," agreed Jason as the duo began walking again. "And speaking personally, I can't say as I blame them. I mean, in the Bible even God admitted it, right there in black and white. If mankind can come together, united as one, then nothing will be impossible for us. Anything we imagine, we can have."

"I'm sorry," said Tom dubiously. "I just can't accept that."

"Can you accept that millions of people vanished without a trace?" countered Jason.

The remark silenced Tom. He hated to admit it, but Jason had a point. The two walked along in renewed silence for a few minutes before Tom posed another of his many questions.

"So," he asked, "why didn't you let them put the goggles on you, Jason? Why don't you have the sign of 666, and why aren't you on their side, ready to join in and create a new world?"

Jason thought for a moment. "I guess I was just lucky," he said at length. "I was too scared to even get close to those goggles. And once I saw what happened to the people who did put them on . . . well, you know what became of Calvin." Jason pursed his lips with determination. "It may be a confusing world out here," he said, "but there is one thing I'm absolutely sure of. Anyone who lets those things get over his eyes comes out twisted and evil."

Tom had to agree. He gave a low whistle. "One thing's for sure," he observed. "Eileen sure had this stuff nailed down tight."

"I'm not sure I follow you," replied a puzzled Jason.

"Think about it," Tom continued. "Look around. It's all happening, just like she said it would. The final battle of God and Satan. The Rapture. The mark of the Beast. It's what she was trying to tell us all along. If only we had listened. I can't remember how many times we teased her about her faith, demanding that God just come out and show Himself for our edification. As if that's what it would take for us to believe."

"Yeah," Jason agreed with regret. "I guess we did."

"And now it's all up front and out in the open," Tom added, sharing his brother-in-law's sadness. "And look where we've ended up. I guess that just goes to show that we were asking the wrong question all along."

"And what was the right question?" Jason wanted to know.

"The only one that matters," Tom replied. "Does God exist? The way I look at it, we assumed that if we knew God existed, that would be enough to satisfy His requirements. But it wasn't because that was the wrong question to begin with. The real question was, Do you believe what He says? Do you accept God for who He is—the Creator of the universe? Look around you, buddy. Everyone knows He exists tonight. And ninety-five percent of the entire world has decided to make war on Him."

The path on which they walked suddenly opened onto a

familiar street. Tom looked at Jason, who returned the stare with a questioning look. Without quite being aware of where they had been headed during their intense conversation, Tom and Jason had returned to the village where Calvin lived. Both of them shared the same unspoken conviction: it was almost as if they had been guided back to this spot.

Chapter

THE SAME HARVEST MOON that had lit the way for Tom and Jason's travels through the forest shone in from the skylight of the penthouse headquarters of Zack Probert and his O.N.E. enforcers. But somehow the light that had been a guiding beacon for the pair now turned into a sinister and menacing illumination on the terrifying scene unfolding in the huge room below, empty except for the large conference table with its model of Babel's tower and a chair to which a woman had been cruelly tied.

The captive lifted her head slowly, dazed and frightened as she heard the sound of a door opening from across Probert's cold and musty lair. With her eyes closed tightly she muttered a few quick words under her breath as the ominous footsteps came closer. When they stopped directly in front of her, she opened her eyes again, only to see the image she had most dreaded: Zack Probert, with Carl and Morgan at his side, holding a pair of the goggles in his black-gloved hand.

"Welcome to your worst nightmare, Queen of Haters," he sneered.

"A nightmare that is only just beginning," added Carl.

"We've got a long night ahead of us, Sweetheart," was Morgan's cruel comment.

"So I think we'd better get started," Carl said.

They moved toward her helpless body, but Probert held up his hand, stopping both men in their tracks. Taking a step toward Helen, he put a finger under her chin and lifted her face to meet his black eyes. "Well, well, well, Miss Helen Hannah," he murmured. "It looks like the time has come for you to find out exactly how much faith you have." Helen only stared back at him, disdaining to reply. "This should be a piece of cake for you," Probert continued. "All you have to do is ask your precious Savior to come and deliver you. Isn't that right?"

He stepped back as if waiting for something to happen. "Oh," he continued at length. "That's a shame. He doesn't seem to hear you. I wonder where He is?"

With a sudden vicious motion he slapped Helen across the face and leaned in close. "I'll tell you where He is. He's running away with His tail between His legs like the filthy coward He is. How can you expect Him to help you when He can't even help Himself?"

Helen still sat silently. After a moment, Probert seemed to tire of his diabolical game. Wordlessly he lifted the goggles high over the head of the helpless Helen Hannah before clamping them down hard. So satisfied was he with his handiwork that he didn't notice Helen turning to the lapel of her jacket and whispering a quick and urgent message.

"I'm in," she said before her body suddenly convulsed

as if from an electric shock and then went completely limp against her bonds.

The darkness of night vanished for Helen, as she stood untied and free from any bruises or other signs of the manhandling she had received, in a world of utter and complete whiteness. In the absence of any dimension, Helen felt dizzy and disoriented until a gentle hand was laid on her shoulder from behind.

"Welcome, Helen Hannah," said the voice of Franco Macalousso, "to your Day of Wonder."

Helen spun around, looking the false messiah straight in the eye and brushing his hand from her shoulder like a bothersome insect. "It's not going to work," she said boldly. "So don't even try it."

"Oh," objected Macalousso with an evil smile, "but it most certainly is going to work. Don't for a minute think that because your great God has won a single little battle the whole war is over. No," he said, wagging his finger in her face. "Don't delude yourself. And never, never underestimate what I am capable of. Tonight the whole world will willingly join my side, Helen Hannah. And as for those who refuse to join my cause, even they shall be given unto me. For you see, united together, mankind is too powerful a force to resist."

Helen lifted her chin high in defiance. "You're forgetting one key thing, Satan," she said, boldly declaring the truth to his face. "Even one soul that trusts in God is a majority. You may be able to unite every mind in the whole world. You can meditate and chant for all you're worth. But when it comes right down to the fundamentals, one soul—one soul that believes and has faith in God—is more powerful than all the armies of your hell and all the deceived minds that are under your spell. Even more powerful than you, Satan."

Macalousso nodded, giving Helen grudging respect. "Revelation 13," he said. "Do I really need to remind you: 'And all the world wondered after the beast . . . and they worshiped the beast saying, Who is like unto the beast?" . . . And it was given unto him to make war with the saints, and to overcome them.'"

Helen's eyes blazed as she answered his blasphemy. "It may be true that you have power over our earthly bodies," she admitted. "But that's not what this is about, is it, Lucifer? You want our souls, but you can't have them unless we freely give them to you. That's what the real battle, and the real war, is about, isn't it? So why bother fighting for something that you know you'll never have? You can't win. It has already been decided."

Macalousso's veneer of civility and charm seemed to evaporate under the assault of Helen's words. His face grew dark, and his eyes began to burn like glowing embers. "Don't lecture me about the battle," he hissed. "You don't understand what is at stake here. Everyone who takes my mark will be mine forever. And you can be assured, I will require the presence of them all when I reign over the eternal lake of fire." He raised his finger to the sky like a twisted symbol of rebellion. "Every soul that I claim is another one lost to Him. And that, for me, is the greatest victory, the sweetest triumph, of them all."

He sneered, his teeth suddenly grown long and sharp behind his thin lips. "Do you think I care about these pathetic creatures?" He laughed, a sound of pure echoing evil. "They are nothing to me but meaningless pawns in a battle as old as time itself."

With a quick nod, Macalousso summoned a pair of guards who wheeled a shiny silver guillotine into the white void. "I once sat up there in heaven's vault itself," he said with vile and bitter rancor. "I was right by His side . . . the most glorious angel in all of creation. I was the very apple of His eye. Until that day, that fateful day, when I committed the unpardonable sin of knowing that I could be like Him. As great and as powerful and as worshiped by the paltry creatures He made in His own image."

"You're nothing like Him, Satan," Helen shot back defiantly, trembling as the guards hauled her to the guillotine and, forcing her to kneel, placed her head beneath the gleaming blade. "God loves the world. He died to save His whole creation. All you want is the world to die for you. You're interested only in deceiving people into giving up their eternal souls so that you can have your vengeance on God."

Macalousso's demonic laughter resounded through the vast white expanse. "Yes," he said, "isn't it wonderful? Already ninety-five percent of the world bear the mark of 666. But tonight, my real victory will be complete. Just imagine, Helen Hannah, all those poor, deluded souls actually believing that they are going to be united in a common purpose, believing that a great divine power is about to be unleashed in them. Pity that they will never know they are rejecting God until it is too late . . . much too late. And when that rejection comes, nothing will ever be the same again. The gates of hell, my kingdom, will open wide, and the real war against the saints of God will commence. We shall never rest until every last one of them is exterminated!"

"You really think you're in control?" Helen said with determined calm as the guards adjusted the clamp around her neck. "I pity you, Satan. There's one thing you have just never understood, and that's that God has given us all, every man and woman, the freedom to choose our destiny for ourselves."

Macalousso reached out and grabbed hold of the release lever on the execution machine. "Well, then," he proclaimed, "I guess the time has come for you to choose."

"I made my choice a long time ago." Helen's last words rang out as the shimmering blade made its fatal descent.

Chapter 14

CALVIN GROANED AS CONSCIOUSNESS slowly returned, and he opened his eyes to find himself lying prone on his living room floor, his head throbbing from the large goose egg that Tom had delivered with the butt of his gun. Slowly rising, first to his hands and knees then finally to his shaky feet, he took a moment to reorient himself and piece together what had happened between him and his brother. Knowing there was no avoiding what he had to do, he crossed to the telephone table and quickly punched up a series of numbers.

"Hello?" he said after too few rings. "Yes. This is Calvin Canboro. No, sir. I'm afraid he . . . got away." He listened for a moment, his face growing ashen from what he heard coming through the line. "Of course, sir," he said at last in a shaky voice. "I'll put them on immediately." Hanging up the phone, he reached for the goggles on the floor and slipped them over his head.

Instantaneously transported to the white realm of Franco Macalousso, Calvin could hear nothing but the beating of his own heart, and he waited in dread for his master to speak.

"Hello, Calvin," came the voice of Franco Macalousso at last.

Calvin cowered at the sound. "Forgive me, Messiah," he whimpered. "I have failed you. I let one of the haters get away."

"Yes," replied Macalousso in a tone of voice that revealed nothing. "Indeed, you have failed me. And not just me, but all your brothers and sisters around the world who are waiting to be united." The pounding of Calvin's heart was louder now and faster, and he was beginning to have trouble breathing. "You see, Calvin," Macalousso continued, "you happen to have let the wrong one slip through your fingers."

Outside Calvin's house, Tom and Jason were approaching stealthily across the front lawn.

"I'm telling you, Tom," Jason was saying in a whisper. "It's too late. Calvin has already made his final choice."

"Maybe that's true," Tom allowed, "and maybe it's not. All I know is that he's my brother, and I've got to try to help him."

"Believe me," pleaded Jason, "it's a waste of time."

Tom signaled for his brother-in-law to hang back as he approached the picture window in the front room. Peering in, he saw the contorted, tortured face of Calvin as he sat on the floor with the goggles clamped over his head. He looked as though he were being skinned alive.

Inside the white world, Calvin thought his heart was

about to burst from his chest. "There is going to be a great battle, Calvin," Macalousso was saying. "And you must understand that unless you're doing everything in your power to further our victory, you are worse than useless to me. And we all know what happens to those who are no longer of use to our great crusade."

Unable to bear watching the pain that racked Calvin's face, Tom rushed to the front door and grabbed the handle. It was locked. Pushing with all his weight, he tried to shoulder it open, but when it still wouldn't budge, he stood back and delivered a resounding kick. As he rushed into the room, Calvin seemed to be in the throes of a fatal heart attack. His body was stiff as a board, and his breathing was coming in great ragged gasps. Putting his ear to his brother's chest, Tom could hear the sound of his heart beating like a scared rabbit, and in the next moment, with a final lunge for air, Calvin lay limp in his arms. Inside the world of the goggles, the infinite whiteness began fading quickly to gray and then to total and impenetrable blackness.

"Calvin!" shouted the grief-stricken Tom as he held his brother on the floor. "Calvin! No! I understand what's going on now," he cried, choking back tears. "Eileen was right . . . she was right all along." He shook his brother's body again, harder this time, but it was too late. Calvin had passed into another reality—one Tom shuddered to think about.

Closing the bulging dead eyes with his fingers, Tom gently laid his brother back down on the floor. His mind was in utter turmoil. What good was all his newfound knowledge if he couldn't help to save the lives of those he cared the most about? Then he noticed a strange wisp of white smoke leaking out from under the collar of Calvin's shirt. Quickly unbuttoning it, he revealed a dark bruise in the precise shape of a hand across Calvin's chest and directly over his heart. Picking up Calvin's hand, he stared with fresh hatred at the 666 emblazoned there. Turning to a framed picture of Franco Macalousso on a nearby table, he muttered a dark curse and added, "So this is the reward you give your faithful followers. I can only imagine what must be in store for your enemies."

He looked sadly down at Calvin's face, still twisted with the agony of his painful death. *Why,* he cried out from the depths of his spirit, *didn't we listen to Eileen when we still had a chance to make the right choice and avoid the deception and despair that are the fruits of Macalousso's rebellion against God?* His deep and soul-searching anguish came to an abrupt end when, from outside the smashed front door, he heard the unmistakable sound of a slamming car door and the pounding of boots along the front porch planks. Catching a glimpse of shadows in the entryway, cast in the ghostly light of the moon, Tom sprang up and, with a few swift steps, bounded up the stairs seconds before Zack Probert, Morgan, and Carl pushed their way into the house.

In the hallway leading to the upstairs bedrooms, Tom stopped, breathing heavily as he listened to Probert bark out instructions to his men. "Search the house," he commanded. "Top to bottom."

Knowing that he had only a matter of a few heartbeats

to escape, Tom looked around desperately for an exit route. A small window at the end of the corridor was sealed tight. Breaking it would certainly attract unwelcome attention. Behind him, he heard the same clump of boots, this time mounting the stairs. With not a second left to spare he slipped into the hallway closet, his gun drawn and ready.

Peering through the louvers of the closet door, he watched with bated breath as Morgan and Carl moved deliberately through the upstairs, checking every nook and cranny. While Morgan searched the bedroom, peering under the bed and behind the chest of drawers, Carl continued looking farther down the hall in the bathroom. Both turning up empty-handed, they met back in the hallway, just outside Tom's tenuous hiding place.

What Tom didn't know was that he was being protected for a purpose and special destiny he could never have guessed at. While he peered fearfully through the closet door, expecting at any moment to be discovered, all that Morgan and Carl saw as they passed by was a blank wall where the door had been. It seems that the element of supernatural warfare had escalated to a new and miraculous level.

Downstairs, Probert waited impatiently for his men to return. Noticing the body of Calvin for the first time, he crossed over and knelt down to pull up the dead man's shirt, revealed the lurid handprint burned onto his chest. Smiling wickedly, he said to himself, "Looks like someone pushed the messiah's patience just a little too far."

Coming up from the basement, Morgan shook his head and tried to still the flutter in his heart. He had found nothing and knew that his superior would not tolerate hearing much more in the way of failure and bad news. At that moment, Carl emerged from the back of the house, a cell phone at his ear. He nodded, then hung up and turned to Probert.

"The haters have taken our bait and fallen in the trap, sir," he reported.

"The transmitter?" Probert asked anxiously, knowing that he, too, would be required to account for his performance before an unforgiving taskmaster.

"Yes, sir," replied Carl crisply. "It happened about an hour ago. They apparently stole it from the satellite station at Fonthill."

"Excellent" was Probert's pleased reply. "No doubt they will soon realize what they have in their hands and the power at their disposal. Then it will be only a matter of time before they attempt to make use of it. I'm willing to bet they will try to interrupt the messiah's message of peace to the world tonight with one of their hate-filled tirades."

At the top of the stairs, Tom, who had hesitantly left his hiding place after the thugs had passed him by, felt his heart freeze at Morgan's smug response to Probert's prediction.

"To do that," he said with a smirk, "they're going to need the help of little Suzie Canboro."

It was all Tom could do to keep from rushing the men, gun blazing, at the menacing suggestion that his wife was about to be the victim of Macalousso and his minions. But he held himself back, listening hard and turning over his next move in his racing mind.

"Is everything set?" Probert asked.

"Absolutely, sir," replied Carl.

"It better be," Probert warned.

"As soon as the satellite detects their signal," Morgan interjected, "we'll be able to pinpoint their exact location. Our men are standing by to move out on a moment's notice."

Although Tom couldn't see Morgan pull a small black box the size of a TV remote control from his suit jacket, his words rang out loud and clear in the dim shadows of the upstairs hallway. "As long as we can put this baby within a hundred miles of their location, we'll be able to jam their broadcast before their disgusting message can reach a single soul."

The conversation was interrupted by the arrival of a uniformed O.N.E. enforcer. "Sir," he said, turning to Probert with a sharp salute, "our communications monitoring network has picked up an unauthorized transmission." He hesitated for a moment, reluctant to reveal the next piece of information. Swallowing hard, he pushed on: "It . . . seems to have originated from your own headquarters, sir. It was rather a large data stream, and the technicians at the base seem to believe that it may have been the work of the hater Helen Hannah. They haven't got it unscrambled yet, but they seem to think it may be in an audio and video mode."

Zack Probert's face twisted with hatred and anger at the news. "And this signal," he said in a low tone as if trying with all his strength to keep from strangling this bearer of bad tidings, "where was its target?"

The officer took an involuntary step backward, his face draining of all color. "They . . . um . . . couldn't locate that . . . I mean . . . not exactly, sir. Although they assure us they're still working on it." He blinked back his growing sense of apprehension. "Whoever was receiving this particular signal went to a lot of trouble to ensure that no one would be able to trace it. But we have determined this much. It was aimed for somewhere out near Rat Lake."

From Tom's perch at the top of the stairs, the name of his and Suzie's favorite getaway spot sent a tingle up his spine. "The cottage," he whispered to himself. If Suzie were anywhere to be found, it would be at their cottage at Rat Lake. He had to get there . . . and get there quickly.

But he could do nothing until Probert and his thugs left and the coast was clear. "Rat Lake, you say?" were the bald, jackbooted bully's next words. "Then we better get ourselves out to Rat Lake on the double, gentlemen."

Turning to the O.N.E. officer, he snapped, "What are you waiting for, you moron? Call for backup immediately."

Tom could vividly picture Probert rubbing his hands together in vile anticipation as he spoke again. "It looks like we won't have to wait for that transmission, after all," he sneered. "Miss Helen Hannah—excuse me, the late Miss Helen Hannah—has done a final service for our glorious messiah. And now it's my turn to render honor to our lord by slaughtering these traitors, one by one."

Tom waited, poised to bolt as he heard the squad of savage killers leave the house, their boots crunching on the gravel driveway as they got into their cars and roared away into the night, sirens wailing. He was about to leap down the stairs, three at a time, when he happened to catch sight of the closet where he had hidden. He allowed himself a moment to ponder how in the world—or in heaven—did they miss him in so obvious a hiding place?

Rushing out the front door, he headed straight toward Calvin's garish purple Volkswagen, jumping in and reaching for the glove compartment where he knew he would find the spare set of keys his late brother always kept handy. A sudden quiet stirring from the backseat of the car caused him to whip around and aim the gun into the shadows of the cramped Beetle.

"Don't . . . shoot . . . ," a familiar voice whined. Jason's face materialized in the gloom. "It's just me, Tom."

Tom shoved the key in the ignition and the engine roared to life. "Where are we going?" Jason asked helplessly.

"No time to explain now," Tom snapped and, spitting gravel from beneath the tires, sent the car fishtailing out the driveway. Just as he was about to pull onto the road leading out of town and up toward the mountain resort of Rat Lake, an idea suddenly struck him. "Wait here," he barked to Jason as he hit the brakes and flung open the door.

Jason watched, mystified, as Tom ran back into Calvin's house, emerging a moment later with a box marked DAN-GER, EXPLOSIVES under his arm. Tossing it into the backseat, he once again headed for the front door. As a seasoned policeman, he had learned the hard way that there was no such thing as too much firepower.

Chapter

THE MOON SHONE BRIGHTLY on the placid surface of the lake, surrounded by tall pines and set in pristine mountain scenery. The soft sound of small lapping waves blended with the rustle of leaves in fragrant wind, and a night owl winged its way against a brilliant background of stars, venturing out for the evening's hunt.

Nestled in a clearing by the lake, where a boat lay tied to a small dock, was a rustic cabin. The gentle glow of lights leaked from its curtained windows. It was a place of perfect peace and tranquillity, except that beyond the log walls of the vacation hideaway, the tension hovered as thickly as the smoke that rose from the burning logs through the river-stone chimney.

Suzie Canboro, Jake Goss, and another key member of their team—an energetic and engaging black woman named Selma Davis—sat around a rough-hewn table deep in discussion. Behind them, three other fugitives from the new world of Franco Macalousso monitored transmission equipment that was scattered around the high-ceilinged cabin. Despite all the activity taking place, a palpable air of gloom hung over the cabin.

"There's got to be a way," Jake was saying, even as he placed his head in his hands with exhausted resignation. "What we've got to figure out is how to uplink for a global broadcast."

"We may never get another chance to reach this many people all at one time," said one of the technicians over her shoulder.

Selma nodded in agreement. "The way Macalousso's been promoting this broadcast, I very much doubt that there's a single soul on earth who won't be watching. Why, I even heard he was setting up viewing stations in the jungles of Africa with simultaneous translators on hand for every language and dialect."

Suzie listened in silence, absently turning the wedding band on her ring finger as she pondered the problems and potentials they faced in the next few hours. When she finally added her thoughts to the general mix, she couldn't hide the discouragement she was feeling. "I don't know," she said with a sigh. "I just don't know if we can do this."

Jake threw a quick look at his wristwatch. "Well," he remarked, "if we are going to do it, we better do it soon." He smiled, trying to convey an optimism he didn't exactly feel. "Let's keep thinking. There's got to be a way to crack this."

"Helen was sure convinced that there was," Selma replied. "She was talking about this exact thing all last week."

"That's right," agreed Jake, then turned to Suzie. "Where is Helen, anyway? Shouldn't she be back by now?"

"I was thinking the same thing," said Suzie, fighting the uneasy feeling that came with the prolonged absence of her friend and partner. "When was the last time we heard from her? Did she check in on schedule?"

"It was right before the last uplink," Selma informed her, then smiled and put her hand over Suzie's. "Try not to worry, girl. Everything's going to work out. I'm believing God for it."

"Well," interjected Jake, "let's hope God makes His move and gets Helen back here pronto. Because I tell you the truth right now: whatever it was she had in mind to do tonight, I'm sure I don't know what it might have been."

In the darkness outside the cabin, on a winding road leading up to the idyllic mountain lake, the twin headlights of a small car were clearly visible against the inky backdrop of the heavy forest. The unlikely sight of a bright purple Volkswagen making its slow way up the ascent startled more than one deer and rabbit who had come down to the road on their way to their nocturnal feeding grounds.

In the driver's seat, Tom peered into the darkness, watching impatiently for the turnoff that led to the Rat Lake road and the Canboro cabin. Beside him was an unusually silent and well-behaved Jason, who seemed for once to realize that the best way he could be of help was to let Tom think without interruption.

At last the small wooden sign pointing to the lake appeared in the headlights. Five minutes later, Tom had parked the car beneath a tall grove of trees and was heading down the path that led to the cabin, with Jason right behind him.

"I just hope we're not too late," Tom was saying. "We've got—"

The sound of gunfire ripped through the silence of the mountain night, and both Tom and Jason stopped dead in their tracks. "Suzie!" Tom cried, forcing the words around the lump in his throat. In the next second, he took off down the trail at full tilt with his brother-in-law doing his best to keep pace.

As he ran, every muscle straining to reach his goal, Tom heard another shot, then another . . . and another. With each deathly echo the anguish on his face intensified. His only thought was for his wife, and the possibility that one of those bullets might be meant for her was more than he could endure. He kept up his headlong pace until, drenched with sweat and gasping for air, he stumbled and went sprawling onto the dirt and pine needle carpet of the forest floor.

A moment later, Jason was by his side, trying to keep him down and out of sight as Tom struggled to rise. The gunshots continued to blaze around them.

"Wait a minute, Tom!" Jason pleaded and pointed in a direction to the left of their position. "The shots . . . they're coming from over there," he continued. He moved his arm until it was parallel with the path down which they had run. "The cabin . . . it's over that way. From across the lake. They're echoes from the other side."

Tom looked up at his brother-in-law. He was right!

Suzie was safe, at least for the moment. Still, with gunfire sounding in this peaceful setting, something must be terribly wrong, and Tom was willing to wager it had something to do with Probert and his men. There wasn't a moment to waste. Struggling to his feet and not bothering to dust the soil and leaves from his clothes, Tom took off once more for the cabin, Jason by his side.

Because of the crackling fire and hum of machinery, the small team of insurgents inside the cabin had not heard the sound of gunshots echoing in the distance. Instead, they were engrossed with the display on a computer terminal that kept flashing *Access Denied* with maddening regularity.

"It's no use," said the technician at the keyboard. "That satellite is locked up tighter than a drum. Unless we can somehow get ahold of that password, we'll never—"

He was interrupted by a commotion at the door as a breathless Tom, followed by an equally winded Jason, burst into the cabin. For a long moment everything else seemed to melt away as Suzie locked eyes with the husband whom she had almost given up hope of ever seeing again. In Tom's expression she could read the same mixture of exuberant joy and deep and humble gratitude to the God who had destined this reunion to come about, regardless of the obstacles and dangers that presented themselves at every turn. Without ever taking their eyes from each other they moved, as if floating on a cloud, to meet in the warmest embrace of their lives. All around them the faces of their friends and fellow warriors for righteousness glowed with the joy they shared with Tom and Suzie Canboro.

"Oh, Suzie," Tom said as he breathed deeply the fragrance of her hair. "I never thought I'd see you again. But here you are in my arms. It's like a prayer has been answered . . . and I didn't even know I was praying."

"He heard you," Suzie whispered, feeling the strength and security of his arms around her. "And He answered you."

She began to cry, but even before the tears could well up and flow down her cheeks, Tom had pulled away, a look of desperate urgency on his face. "We've got to get out of here," he told her.

Turning to the others, he repeated, "We've all got to get out of here now. Macalousso and his goons know about this place. They're over on the other side of the lake right now, going from cabin to cabin shooting anything and everything that moves. They may not find this place for a little while longer but eventually—"

Before Tom could finish his warning, a man decked out in a pitch-black O.N.E. uniform, complete with a flak vest and gloves, burst into the room, an automatic weapon leveled at its occupants.

"Well, well, well," he snarled. "What have we here? This must be the rest of Helen Hannah's ugly little nest of crawling haters."

Striding through the room as everyone stood frozen in place, he headed straight for a Bible on a desk near the broadcast equipment. Picking it up and holding it out to the others like a piece of roadkill, he taunted them. "So," said the O.N.E. officer, "is this what it's supposed to be about for you haters? Some little fairy tale, written by a bunch of ignorant fishermen two thousand years ago? You think this book is going to be the answer to all your questions?" He laughed, a vicious unbridled sound. "Well, I've got news for you all. Today's the day for you to answer the biggest question of them all." Pulling back the hammer of his gun, he thought for a moment, then picked Tom out from the rest. Striding up to his intended victim, he put the barrel of the gun against Tom's temple and leaned in close to whisper in his ear. "Are you ready to die for what you believe?"

When Tom remained silent, the man turned to the others and shouted out the same question: "Are any of you ready to die for what you believe?" One by one he pointed the weapon at them, and with only one exception, they met his threat with a calm assurance that spoke loudly and clearly of their answer to his lethal question. The one exception was Jason, who looked so terrified Tom was afraid for a moment that he would faint dead away.

"Just as I thought," the O.N.E. cop continued. "You all talk so tough about how you're going to keep our messiah from fulfilling his mission. You tell the world that only you have the way, the truth, and the light. Well, let's see how tough you talk now—with your lives on the line."

Returning the gun to Tom's head, he asked again, "How about you? Are you ready to die for God?"

"No . . . please," Suzie began to plead, but a single look from her husband silenced her.

Looking straight into his wife's eyes the whole time he spoke, Tom began his words in a low, soft voice that gradually rose in strength and conviction as he felt the power of his faith surge up inside him. "I never truly understood God's love," he began, "until I saw my brother die without it. Until I saw this whole world trying to live without it. All I can think of to do right now is to thank God for giving me another chance to accept Him . . . to believe Him." He turned to his tormentor. "Go ahead and do whatever you have to do, Officer," he concluded, his eyes burning with fervor. "But I'll tell you one thing right now. You're too late."

"Oh, am I?" came the response as the cop suddenly turned the gun away from Tom and pointed it straight at his beloved wife. In response, she crossed over to her husband, and together they stood, arm in arm, side by side. A long moment passed. One after another, the occupants of the cabin stepped forward. First Selma. Then Jake. Then the others. At last they stood facing the barrel of the gun—all except Jason.

The cop grinned. "I don't blame you, pal," he said. "What book of old fairy tales is worth dying for, anyway?"

Jason turned frantically, first to his sister, then to his brother-in-law, and then back to the gun poised in the man's hand. He started to tremble, then suddenly broke down sobbing. "I can't do it," he wailed. "I'm sorry . . . I . . . just . . . can't do it!"

"Then I suggest you take a hike before the bullets start flying," the O.N.E. officer commanded. With that, Jason bolted out the door followed by the cry of his sister, begging him to stop and come back.

With his hands over his ears to block the sound of Suzie's pleas, Jason stumbled into the darkness, tripping over the root of a tree and running blindly into the forest. But no matter how hard he clamped shut his ears, there was no way to keep out the sound of shots from the cabin, one after the other. In terror and deep shame he fell to his knees, sobbing uncontrollably.

Inside the cabin, however, a far different scene was being played out from the one imagined in Jason's mind. After he fled through the front door, the menacing O.N.E. officer carefully and deliberately emptied the chamber of his gun into the fireplace logs, one after the other. When he had finished, he stepped back and grinned broadly. Taking the glove off his right hand, he held it up for all to see: the mark of the Beast was nowhere in evidence.

"Forgive me for that little charade," he said. "The name's Steve Jones. I had to make sure you were who I thought you were. See, I'm on your side."

It took a moment for this incredible news to sink in to the minds of those who, seconds before, had prepared themselves to die. It took another moment to decide whether to really trust this man who called himself Steve Jones. But the frank and sincere look in his eyes did much to convince them of the truth of his words.

As soon as she had recovered her wits, Suzie rushed to the window to look for her brother. She turned back, fear reigniting in her eyes. "He's taken the van," she said to Tom.

"Don't worry," Tom reassured her. "Believe me, no one is going to be able to catch your brother if he doesn't want to be caught."

Steve Jones cleared his throat to get their attention. "I

hope he'll be all right," he said, referring to Jason, "but I had to be absolutely sure all of you were willing to take the last step to stop Macalousso. See," he continued, pulling a small black box out of his jacket pocket, "I've got something here I think you can use, and I wouldn't want to take the chance of its falling into the wrong hands."

"What is it?" asked Jake curiously.

"It's a way to directly uplink to the main O.N.E. orbiting satellite," explained their new friend.

"You mean," asked one of the incredulous techs, "you've got the access code?"

"Better," replied the smiling Steve Jones, holding up the black box. "With this little contraption you don't need any secret codes or classified frequencies. Just hook up this little critter and you can cut directly into Macalousso's speech. The whole world will hear what you've got to say." He glanced at his watch. "But you better hurry," he urged. "Macalousso is scheduled to go on right about now."

Suzie and Tom traded a glance that expressed the feeling both shared: Could this miraculous turn of events really be true, or was it some new and elaborate deception by the enemy? "Are you sure about this?" Suzie asked after a moment. "I think I'd feel better if Helen were here. She's a lot more knowledgeable about—"

"I'm afraid that won't be possible," said Steve Jones with a somber expression. "You see, Helen Hannah . . . isn't with us anymore."

"God . . . no," cried Suzie and turned for comfort to Tom's arms.

"But how did it happen?" asked an equally shocked Selma.

Steve Jones nodded toward the computer screen. "I think you'll find the answer to that question there," he said, and immediately Jake sat down at the keyboard and began punching out a series of commands.

After a moment, words began unscrolling on the screen. As Jake read them aloud, the only other sound in the room was Suzie's soft sobs. "I have fought the good fight," Jake read. "I have finished my course. I have kept the faith. Please be strong and always remember what we are battling for and who is on our side." He turned to the others. "There's a video file attached," he told them.

"What's on it?" Tom asked Steve, speaking for them all.

"A confession," the newcomer revealed. "Videotaped from the big man himself."

"You mean . . . Macalousso?" Suzie inquired.

"That's right," replied Steve Jones, nodding. "This is what we've all been looking for to show the world who he really is. Even as he's about to announce that he has come to save us all, we can show him in his true colors, thanks to Helen."

"Using that thing?" Tom persisted, pointing to the black box in Steve's hand.

"Exactly," Steve replied. "With this transmitter we can send a signal directly to the O.N.E. satellite. We liberated it earlier this evening from—"

"Don't tell me," Tom interrupted. "From the Fonthill broadcast station."

"How did you know?" asked the mystified Jones.

"It's a trap," Tom told him, then turned to the others. "As soon as we send off that signal, they'll be on us. It'll be like painting a big fat bull's-eye right on the cabin roof."

"But," Suzie ventured, "will our signal get out?"

"If we can show Helen's tape to the world," added Jake, "then it will be worth it."

Tom shook his head sadly. "No deal," he told them. "They've got a jammer. I couldn't tell you what it is, and I sure don't know how it works, but I do know this: they're expecting you to broadcast a signal . . . a signal they have no intention of ever letting get through."

"But there must be a way to stop the jamming," insisted a desperate Selma. "Can't we do something?"

A long silence followed. They had come so far. Would God allow them to fail now? Would Satan emerge triumphant from the greatest battle the world had ever witnessed?

Chapter

Under the dark cover of the mountain night, a squadron of cars pulled up to a ridgeline overlooking the sparkling lake below. Zack Probert emerged from the lead vehicle, followed by a phalanx of heavily armed men. As he watched, Morgan scurried to the top of the nearby knoll and gazed at the valley below through a pair of infrared binoculars.

Scanning the landscape back and forth, he at first noticed nothing unusual and no sign of the heat rays that would indicate the presence of life. Completing his inspection, he called down to his superior. "Nothing down here," he reported.

"Keep looking," Probert commanded, and his lackey was quick to obey.

On his second inspection Morgan caught a faint glimmer behind a stand of pine trees, and using the zoom function on the lenses, he zeroed in on the still-warm emissions from a car engine. An even closer look revealed a telltale VW logo. "Got it," said Morgan and hurried back down to where the others were waiting.

"Time to clean up this world once and for all," Probert

remarked when he heard the news. "Let's take care of this scum."

Not half a mile away, inside the Canboro cabin, Tom and Suzie watched tensely as the technicians hooked up the final wires of an elaborate relay that connected the broadcast equipment to the black transmitter box provided by Steve Jones. At a signal from Jake, Jones threw a small switch on the box at the same time other techs punched a series of buttons, sending instantaneous commands high above the earth's atmosphere where, in the darkness of space, a satellite orbited.

Everyone turned to watch the screen on the cabin's TV as the lights went up and Franco Macalousso was revealed sitting behind a large chromium desk in the hall of a magnificent palace. "Your moment has arrived, Planet Earth," he said, and the power of his voice was as electrifying as the force of his charisma. "Together you and I . . . all of us . . . can and will unleash the power of our united consciousness. Nothing and no one will stand in our way. And nothing that you and I can imagine will be denied to us."

At a computer monitor near the broadcast equipment, Selma awaited her cue from Jake.

"I can feel our power growing," Macalousso was proclaiming. "Together, you and I can rid this world of hatred and fear once and for all. Concentrate, my friends. Believe." He closed his eyes as if to demonstrate. "Awaken within yourselves the powers of our united minds."

"What are we waiting for?" Suzie asked Jake. "We've got to stop him."

"We're ready," he replied. Turning to Selma, he nodded and said, "Go for it."

In the blink of an eye, the image of Macalousso, the very visage of Satan himself as he appeared before Helen Hannah in the vast wasteland of his white world, appeared on the computer monitor.

"Who is that?" asked an astonished Tom.

"That's the image of the Beast," Selma replied grimly. "It's the image Helen gave her life to capture for us and for the whole world. That's what's waiting for anyone who puts on those goggles."

"The image of the Beast?" Tom repeated. "But I don't understand . . ."

"Revelation 13," Selma explained. "'And he had power to give life unto the image of the beast, that the image of the beast should both speak, and cause that as many as would not worship the image of the beast should be killed.'"

Tom's eyes returned to the same sight on the screen that had kept everyone in the room in silent and horrified fascination. Macalousso's image was the very embodiment of pure evil.

"Macalousso tried to infiltrate the resistance with spies who used tiny cameras on their contact lenses," Jake revealed. "Helen must have gotten ahold of one and finally put it to good use."

Suzie nodded. "That must have been her plan from the very beginning," she speculated. "She used herself as bait in order to get close to him . . . to show the world who he really is before it's too late."

"Incredible," Tom said as he beheld the face of God's ancient enemy, revealed for all to see.

While the historic drama played out inside the cabin, another age-old struggle was reaching its conclusion at a small, hidden turnout near the lake. The familiar battered blue van was parked in the shadows, and there, over the sounds of crickets and frogs, a voice could be heard as if crying out a warning in the wilderness.

"They who call upon the name of the Lord shall be saved," Jack Van Impe was saying. "That will be as true in their day as it is in ours."

"Thank you," chimed the voice of Rexella Van Impe. "And I just want to add that it is in my heart today to encourage you all."

Inside the van sat Jason, his head bowed in his hands, weeping like a small child. Before him, two television monitors glowed. On the first, the hellish image of Franco Macalousso. On the other, one of the outlaw videotapes of Jack and Rexella Van Impe.

"No matter where you are," Rexella continued, "no matter what your circumstances, God is greater . . . He loves you and has a plan for your life. Even if you think you've failed God, if you've gone too far down into sin, He is still waiting for you with open arms . . . waiting for you simply to ask."

Jason looked up at the video image of Rexella, and words began to tremble at the edge of his lips.

Nearby, Zack and his men had arrived at the turnout where Tom had hidden Calvin's conspicuous purple

Beetle. With a grin he turned to his thugs and produced a small black box from his pocket. "I guess we won't be needing this jammer after all," he said. "It looks like we've just about run these vermin to ground."

Pulling a large-bore revolver from the holster under his jacket, Probert cocked it and lifted it high over his head. "Gentlemen," he commanded, "the time has come. We go in guns blazing and kill anything and everything that moves."

With Morgan and Carl close behind, Zack strode up the steps of the cabin, landing a deafening kick on the door with his boot. "Adios, haters!" he shouted.

The three men burst through the front door, guns erupting in fire and smoke. But it took no more than a second for the shock of their situation to register. Far from a room full of helpless victims, Zack and the others had stumbled into a trap cleverly laid by Tom from the moment he had arrived at the lake. Leaving the car parked near another cabin down the road from the Canboro place, Tom and Jason had carefully booby-trapped the place with the dynamite and plastic explosives taken from Calvin's home. All it would take was the front door opening to set the fuse, and the job would be complete.

From the window of his cabin through the pine forest, Tom watched as a tremendous fireball erupted in the woods and flaming debris began falling from the sky. The concussion of the explosion hit a moment later, rocking the house. When it was over, he turned back to the others and shouted, "Okay! Let's do it! Now!"

Jake wasted no time. Hitting the switch, he watched as the rolling tape got up to speed. "This'll just take a few seconds," he assured the others. "Then we'll be on the air."

From across the room Suzie flipped the switch, activating the frozen frame of Macalousso as Helen had captured him. Immediately all eyes turned to the television broadcast.

"Don't you see," Macalousso was saying into the camera. "All I ever did was to try to tell the world the truth about their situation. And that truth is that we all possess the power to be gods. That's the truth that frightens God so badly that He banished me from heaven itself. But it wasn't just me who was thrown down to the depths below. Oh, no. There were many, many of us. Can't you see? He had to keep us quiet. We knew His secret. So we had no choice but to wage a great war against Him. And now, His only hope is to try to convince all of you that I am nothing but a liar and a deceiver. He would have you believe that if you follow me, you will face an eternity in hell. That is the last desperate lie of a failed and futile God!"

At that precise moment the television screen went blank briefly, then the devilish features of Macalousso appeared as he really was, as Helen had seen him.

"This one's for you, Helen," Suzie whispered under her breath as the tape began to roll.

"Everyone who takes my mark will be mine forever," the tape documented him saying. "And you can be assured, I will require the presence of them all when I reign over the eternal lake of fire." His finger pointed to the sky, a twisted symbol of rebellion. "Every soul that I claim is another one lost to Him. And that, for me, is the greatest victory, the sweetest triumph, of them all."

The screen showed the long and sharp teeth behind his thin lips. "Do you think I care about these pathetic creatures?" His evil laugh echoed over the airwaves. "They are nothing to me but meaningless pawns in a battle as old as time itself."

Down the road, Jason watched the same bizarre spectacle unfolding on the monitor in the van. He listened in awe as Helen's voice rang out loud and clear.

"You're nothing like Him, Satan," she was saying. "God loves the world. He died to save His whole creation. All you want is the world to die for you. You're interested only in deceiving people into giving up their eternal souls so that you can have your vengeance on God."

As Helen spoke the unmistakable message of truth, Jason fell to his knees on the floor of the van. Ripping off the baseball cap on his head, he tore out the foil lining and began slowly and deliberately to pray, his mind clear and uncluttered for the first time in as long as he could remember.

Above him on the screen, Helen's voice was abruptly terminated as the WNN STAND BY slate was put up behind a field of static snow. After a moment Macalousso reappeared in the midst of his magnificent palace, but instead of the confident, charismatic creature from earlier that evening, he had turned into a whining, whimpering old man trying to hold on to the last shred of his illusory power.

"They're at it again," he was saying. "The haters. They'll do anything to fill your minds with fear and disbelief." Under the harsh television lights, he seemed to be shriveling away before the eyes of the world.

"Come on," he begged. "Join with me." He held up an imploring hand. "Wait," he cried. "Don't leave. We need to stand together. Please, stay with me. We were so close. Please . . ."

In the cabin Tom and Suzie stood arm in arm, watching with the others as the pathetic sight of a defeated Lucifer was aired for all the world to see. While the others stared with rapt attention at the television, Tom slipped his hand into his coat pocket and pulled out a small blue box. Taking the diamond ring from inside, he slipped it on his wife's finger as her eyes filled with tears and she lifted her face up to his to share a kiss of love and gratitude.

Epilogue

Dawn was breaking as Tom and Suzie drove together down the mountain toward the lights of the newborn city. Along the roadside they passed by a ramshackle country church, boarded up and condemned by the once omnipotent O.N.E. police. As the sun cracked over the horizon, lighting the pines with a gilded glow, Tom pulled to the side of the road near the church.

"Just give me a minute," he said to his wife.

"Take as long as you need," she replied with a smile.

Entering the church, Tom moved past the ransacked pews and overturned altar, ignoring the spray-painted graffiti that read King of the Haters. Behind him the figures of Suzie and Jason appeared as he approached a broken stained-glass window through which a single beam of light shone.

Tom swallowed hard, and he stared up at the light. His eyes filled with tears of joy and repentance.

"I'm here because I have a promise to keep to my sister," he said in a low voice nearly overcome with emotion.

"And I'm late. I'm really late. But I want to get to know You. I want to learn to open myself up. I'm not good at saying prayers because I never learned how. So I'm going to talk to You like You're right here . . . because now I know You are."

LEFT BEHIND™
THE MOVIE

On the Event Horizon

Taking Off October 31, 2000

Millions of readers have been enraptured
by the wildly popular
Left Behind
book series.

hose same readers have eagerly waited the release
of *Left Behind: The Movie.*

On October 31,
they won't have to wait any longer.